This Is Love

Athina felt her temper rising.

She did not speak, however, but walked towards the door.

"Where are you going?" the Marquess asked as she reached it.

Athina turned back.

"As you have lived up to your reputation, My Lord," she said, "I will tell you exactly where I am going. I am taking the child to Windsor Castle, to the Queen."

If she had thrown a bomb at the Marquess, he could not have been more surprised.

Never in his whole life had a woman spoken to him in such a manner.

It seemed incredible that anyone so small, so fragile and beautiful, should so insult him.

A Camfield Novel of Love
by Barbara Cartland

Camfield Place,
Hatfield
Hertfordshire,
England

Dearest Reader,

Camfield Novels of Love mark a very exciting era of my books with Jove. They have already published nearly two hundred of my titles since they became my first publisher in America, and now all my original paperback romances in the future will be published exclusively by them.

As you already know, Camfield Place in Hertford-shire is my home, which originally existed in 1275, but was rebuilt in 1867 by the grandfather of Beatrix Potter.

It was here in this lovely house, with the best view in the county, that she wrote *The Tale of Peter Rabbit*. Mr. McGregor's garden is exactly as she described it. The door in the wall that the fat little rabbit could not squeeze underneath and the goldfish pool where the white cat sat twitching its tail are still there.

I had Camfield Place blessed when I came here in 1950 and was so happy with my husband until he died, and now with my children and grandchildren, that I know the atmosphere is filled with love and we have all been very lucky.

It is easy here to write of love and I know you will enjoy the Camfield Novels of Love. Their plots are definitely exciting and the covers very romantic. They come to you, like all my books, with love.

Bless you,

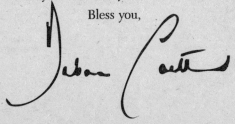

CAMFIELD NOVELS OF LOVE

by Barbara Cartland

THE POOR GOVERNESS
WINGED VICTORY
LUCKY IN LOVE
LOVE AND THE MARQUIS
A MIRACLE IN MUSIC
LIGHT OF THE GODS
BRIDE TO A BRIGAND
LOVE COMES WEST
A WITCH'S SPELL
SECRETS
THE STORMS OF LOVE
MOONLIGHT ON THE
   SPHINX
WHITE LILAC
REVENGE OF THE HEART
THE ISLAND OF LOVE
THERESA AND A TIGER
LOVE IS HEAVEN
MIRACLE FOR A MADONNA
A VERY UNUSUAL WIFE
THE PERIL AND THE
   PRINCE
ALONE AND AFRAID
TEMPTATION OF A
   TEACHER
ROYAL PUNISHMENT
THE DEVILISH DECEPTION
PARADISE FOUND
LOVE IS A GAMBLE
A VICTORY FOR LOVE
LOOK WITH LOVE
NEVER FORGET LOVE
HELGA IN HIDING
SAFE AT LAST
HAUNTED
CROWNED WITH LOVE
ESCAPE
THE DEVIL DEFEATED
THE SECRET OF THE
   MOSQUE
A DREAM IN SPAIN
THE LOVE TRAP
LISTEN TO LOVE
THE GOLDEN CAGE

LOVE CASTS OUT FEAR
A WORLD OF LOVE
DANCING ON A RAINBOW
LOVE JOINS THE CLANS
AN ANGEL RUNS AWAY
FORCED TO MARRY
BEWILDERED IN BERLIN
WANTED—A WEDDING RING
THE EARL ESCAPES
STARLIGHT OVER TUNIS
THE LOVE PUZZLE
LOVE AND KISSES
SAPPHIRES IN SIAM
A CARETAKER OF LOVE
SECRETS OF THE HEART
RIDING IN THE SKY
LOVERS IN LISBON
LOVE IS INVINCIBLE
THE GODDESS OF LOVE
AN ADVENTURE OF LOVE
THE HERB FOR HAPPINESS
ONLY A DREAM
SAVED BY LOVE
LITTLE TONGUES OF FIRE
A CHIEFTAIN FINDS LOVE
A LOVELY LIAR
THE PERFUME OF THE GODS
A KNIGHT IN PARIS
REVENGE IS SWEET
THE PASSIONATE PRINCESS
SOLITA AND THE SPIES
THE PERFECT PEARL
LOVE IS A MAZE
A CIRCUS FOR LOVE
THE TEMPLE OF LOVE
THE BARGAIN BRIDE
THE HAUNTED HEART
REAL LOVE OR FAKE
KISS FROM A STRANGER
A VERY SPECIAL LOVE
THE NECKLACE OF LOVE
A REVOLUTION OF LOVE
THE MARQUIS WINS
LOVE IS THE KEY

LOVE AT FIRST SIGHT
THE TAMING OF A TIGRESS
PARADISE IN PENANG
THE EARL RINGS A BELLE
THE QUEEN SAVES THE
   KING
NO DISGUISE FOR LOVE
LOVE LIFTS THE CURSE
BEAUTY OR BRAINS?
TOO PRECIOUS TO LOSE
HIDING
A TANGLED WEB
JUST FATE
A MIRACLE IN MEXICO
WARNED BY A GHOST
TWO HEARTS IN HUNGARY
A THEATER OF LOVE
A DYNASTY OF LOVE
MAGIC FROM THE HEART
THE WINDMILL OF LOVE
LOVE STRIKES A DEVIL
LOVE AND WAR
SEEK THE STARS
A CORONATION OF LOVE
A WISH COMES TRUE
LOVED FOR HIMSELF
A KISS IN ROME
HIDDEN BY LOVE
BORN OF LOVE
WALKING TO
   WONDERLAND
TERROR FROM THE
   THRONE
THE CAVE OF LOVE
THE PEAKS OF ECSTASY
LUCKY LOGAN FINDS LOVE
THE ANGEL AND THE
   RAKE
THE QUEEN OF HEARTS
THE WICKED WIDOW
TO SCOTLAND AND LOVE
LOVE AT THE RITZ
THE DANGEROUS
   MARRIAGE
GOOD OR BAD?

A NEW CAMFIELD NOVEL OF LOVE BY

BARBARA CARTLAND

This Is Love

J

JOVE BOOKS, NEW YORK

THIS IS LOVE

A Jove Book / published by arrangement with
the author

PRINTING HISTORY
Jove edition / January 1994

ISBN: 0-515-11286-0

A JOVE BOOK®
Jove Books are published by The Berkley Publishing Group,
200 Madison Avenue, New York, New York 10016.
JOVE and the "J" design are
trademarks belonging to Jove Publications, Inc.

PRINTED IN THE UNITED STATES OF AMERICA

10 9 8 7 6 5 4 3 2 1

Author's Note

THE Master of the Horse is esteemed the third great officer at Court, giving place only to the Lord Steward and the Lord Chamberlain of the Household.

Formerly this Officer was called Constable and held much more power than his successors of today.

He now has the charge of ordering and disposing of all matters relating to the Sovereign's stables, races, and breeds of horses, and has jurisdiction over the Equerries, Pages, and others employed in his department.

At State Processions, he rides next behind the Sovereign, and in the case of a Queen Regnant, in the carriage with Her Majesty.

At the Coronation of Queen Victoria, the Master of the Horse and the Mistress of the Robes rode in the State carriage with the Queen.

The present Master is the Duke of Westmoreland.

Historically, records of the appointment started in 1391 with the first Master of the Horse, Sir John Russell.

There were four previous holders of the position, starting in 1360, but Russell was the first to hold the title officially. He served Richard II.

At that time the appointment changed with the Government of the day and was part of the Government Administration.

In the early days he was also Lord High Constable in Battle, besides having jurisdiction over the Royal Stables, race-horses, and Studs.

chapter one

1885

LADY Athina Ling turned her horses off the main road and drove down a narrow lane.

She resented having to slacken their pace because it was growing late and she was still a long way from home.

The hedges were high and she drove carefully.

At the first bend, however, she had hastily to pull sharply at the reins.

Just in front of her, coming out of a field, was a farm-wagon.

The horse was right across the lane.

The farm yokel driving it realised somewhat belatedly that there was other traffic beside himself.

He managed to turn his horse as Lady Athina pulled in hers.

The Chaise would just have had room to pass the farm-wagon if the wagon had been pointing straight up the lane.

As it was, the lighter wheel of the Chaise crashed against that of the wagon.

1

The horses came to a standstill, and the groom with Lady Athina jumped out.

The wheels were fortunately not locked together.

At the same time, the wheel of the Chaise, being the lighter of the two, was somewhat damaged.

"Ye be a-comin' too fast!" the yokel said aggressively, fearing that someone would blame him for what had happened.

"I am afraid I was," Lady Athina replied in a soft voice, "and this lane is very narrow."

"Folks've said that afore," the yokel remarked.

The groom came to the side of the Chaise.

"I'm afraid, M'Lady," he said, "the wheel's damaged. Not badly, but it'd be a mistake to try and get 'ome on it."

"You mean we must have it mended first?" Lady Athina asked.

"If we can find someone to do it."

The yokel was listening.

"There be a blacksmith oop at Crown an' Feathers," he said, "an' a good 'un, if 'e ain't gorn 'ome."

"And where is the Crown and Feathers?" Lady Athina enquired.

He pointed down the lane by which they had just come.

" 'E goes down thar," he said, "'tis th' best Posting-Inn in these parts, and it be on th' left."

"Thank you," Lady Athina said, "now, tell me where I can turn."

He pointed ahead and the groom got into the Chaise.

Very carefully Lady Athina tooled her well-bred horses to where there was a wide entrance into a field.

She turned the Chaise round.

As they went back past the farm-wagon, the wheel was bumping and somewhat unsteady.

"You are quite right, Gauntlet," she said. "We could not get home with it like this."

"I'm afraid it'll take an 'our or so to mend, M'Lady," Gauntlet replied.

"Well, if it does, we will just have to stay the night at the Posting-Inn."

There was silence, and Lady Athina knew that he disapproved of the idea.

Gauntlet had been with her Father since she was a child.

Now that he had died, Gauntlet looked after her as if she were one of his own children.

"It is no use being disapproving," she said after a moment when he did not speak. "I know I should have a Chaperon, but you are far more effective than even Mrs. Beckwith could be."

"People'd be shocked, M'Lady, if they knowed you was a-stayin' in a Public Inn wi'out Mrs. Beckwith in attendance."

Athina laughed, and it was a very pretty sound.

"You are making me sound as if I were Royalty, Gauntlet! It will be only for one night, and if you think it might cause a scandal, I will not use my own name."

She paused before she added:

"I will be 'Mrs. Beckwith'—why not?"

Gauntlet made a sound which signified neither approval nor disapproval.

As she drove on, Athina thought how lucky she was to have him with her.

She could always rely on him in an emergency.

If there were drunken young men at the Inn who insulted her, Gauntlet would deal with them.

The wheel was decidedly more wobbly by the time the Crown and Feathers came into view.

It was, as the yokel had said, a large, impressive Posting-Inn for such a sparsely inhabited part of the country.

Lady Athina was aware that there were no big houses nearby where she might have found friends.

However, to have gone back to where she had come from would have been as far as going home.

She had been staying the night with an ancient Aunt who had been on the verge of death for the last five years.

Athina was quite certain she would last for another five before she finally arrived at the Heaven she was convinced was waiting for her.

In the meantime, she enjoyed more or less compelling her relatives to visit her.

When they arrived, she tantalised them with promises of benefiting from her Will.

Such promises were usually almost rescinded before they left.

As far as Athina was concerned, she wanted nothing from her Aunt.

However, she felt it was her duty to go when she received one of her plaintive letters starting:

"This may be the last time I am able to invite you to visit me."

Athina had enjoyed the drive.

She had been very firm when her Chaperon, Mrs. Beckwith, had suggested accompanying her.

"You know long drives give you a headache," she said, "and that Aunt Muriel will treat you as if you are dust beneath her feet. She has never had any time for what she calls 'superfluous additions to the household,' and that, I am afraid, is the category into which you come."

They both laughed.

"Well, I know that Gauntlet will look after you," Mrs. Beckwith said, "and you will be away for only one night."

"I will be back in time for dinner on Tuesday," Athina promised.

She kissed Mrs. Beckwith affectionately.

When she left she had waved to her as she went down the drive.

Athina's Father, the Earl of Murling, had died last year.

He had left his only child a large fortune, a large house, and a large Estate.

What relatives there were in the vicinity had, immediately after the Funeral, asked Athina with which of them she intended to reside.

Alternatively, who she wished to come to live with her as Chaperon.

"When I looked at their faces," Athina said later to Mrs. Beckwith, "I knew what they were really thinking was how much money Papa had left me, and that it must be kept in the Family."

"That was actually very sensible of them," Mrs. Beckwith replied.

"Not at all," Athina said. "It was sheer greed. They were afraid that I would be pursued by fortune-hunters who would somehow contrive to get their hands on money which might otherwise have been theirs!"

"Now you are being cynical," Mrs. Beckwith demurred. "You are too young, Dearest, and too beautiful to look at the world through anything except rose-coloured glasses."

"I think, if nothing else, Papa taught me to be practical," Athina replied, "and I know that another way in which I resemble him is that I dislike being bored by people who do not use their brain and whose only conversation is local gossip."

Mrs. Beckwith laughed again.

She was a very attractive widow nearing forty, who had been one of Athina's Tutors.

The Earl, who deeply regretted that he had no son, was a very intelligent man.

He had his daughter educated so that she would be able to converse with him on level terms.

She had had, of course, a Governess, but she had played only a small part in her education.

She had, in addition, Tutors in all the main subjects that her Father considered were important for a man.

Mrs. Beckwith was an acknowledged expert in Geography.

She had travelled a great deal with her husband, who had been a Medical Missionary.

She had written a book which had a fair amount of success.

When her husband was killed by cannibals, she came back to England.

She lived here with her Father, who was the Bishop of Oxford.

When the Earl heard of her reputation, he had asked her to come to Murling Park and stay for two nights every week.

During that time she taught Athina.

The lessons had proved an enormous success.

Mrs. Beckwith was an extraordinarily clever teacher.

Athina enjoyed travelling with her in thought and imagination as she hoped one day to travel in reality.

Athina's Father had died just before she was eighteen.

She was now a very well-educated and intelligent young woman.

The Earl had arranged for her to be presented at Court and to have her first Season in London.

But as she was plunged into mourning, it was obviously impossible that summer.

This year, however, the Family had agitated and arranged that she should go to London at the beginning of May.

That was now about two weeks ahead.

Athina was already wondering if she really wished to leave the country.

"I love being here when there are primroses in the hedgerows and daffodils in the Park," she said to Mrs. Beckwith. "I cannot believe that anything in London could be more entrancing."

"You know as well as I do," Mrs. Beckwith replied, "that you have to meet charming young men, dance every night at a Ball, and fulfill your Father's dream that you will be the 'Belle of the Season.' "

Athina laughed.

"Papa wanted me to be that because it would be a compliment to him! He always behaved as if he had created me."

"Which of course he had!" Mrs. Beckwith smiled. "If he were here now, I would certainly congratulate him!"

Athina laughed again.

"I have the uncomfortable feeling that both you and Papa are going to be disappointed," she said. "What will happen is that the young men I meet will think I am a 'blue stocking' and avoid me like the Plague!"

Mrs. Beckwith put her head on one side and contemplated her pupil.

"I have actually wondered about that myself," she confessed. "You must, Athina, be intelligent enough to let the man always know best."

Athina threw up her hands.

"I refuse! I absolutely refuse!" she declared. "If they say something stupid, as some of Papa's friends used to do, I shall find it impossible not to correct them."

"In which case you will have to come home and talk to the primroses and the daffodils," Mrs. Beckwith warned her.

"And, of course, you, Dearest Becky," Athina added. "I love talking to you, and that reminds me, that new book on the Universe has just arrived and we must both read it tonight."

The Library at Murling Park was already packed with new books.

Athina was far more interested in them than in the clothes she had been buying to take to London.

She had wanted to rent a house in Mayfair and stay there on her own with Mrs. Beckwith.

But there was such an outcry from her relations at such an idea that she agreed instead to stay with one of her Aunts.

This particular Aunt was married to a Gentleman-in-Waiting at Buckingham Palace.

She therefore had the *entree* to all the important functions there.

Mrs. Beckwith had agreed to stay behind in the country, and Athina knew she would miss her.

She was still rather dubious as to what she would find in the Social World, how it could compare with the joy of owning the finest stables in the country.

There were also her Father's horses still at New-market.

It had been impossible while she was in mourning to attend Race-Meetings.

Queen Victoria had set the fashion for long-drawn-out and over-emphasised black mourning after she lost her beloved Prince Albert.

Athina had therefore been confined to Murling Park.

It had not troubled her in the slightest.

She missed her Father—it would have been impossible not to do so.

But Mrs. Beckwith was an amusing and delightful companion.

The horses, Athina often thought, compensated for having no young men to talk to.

She looked wonderful as she rode off on some spirited horse which she quickly had under control that Mrs. Beckwith would watch her and sigh.

Athina was so lovely with her golden curls which had a touch of red in them.

Her grey eyes were unusual.

In fact, she had a beauty that made her different from all other girls of her age.

It was, Mrs. Beckwith knew, the reason why she had been christened Athina, after the Greek goddess.

From the moment she was born she had a loveliness few other babies had.

"I wonder what will happen to her?" Mrs. Beckwith asked herself as Athina trotted down the drive.

Her sylph-like figure was silhouetted against the darkness of the trees.

The way she rode reminded her of Diana the Huntress.

Now Athina drove her horses into a large courtyard.

There were several carriages of different sorts parked at one end.

This meant that the horses had already been taken into the stables and their owners had gone into the Inn.

"Do not forget that I am 'Mrs. Beckwith,'" Athina warned Gauntlet as she drew the horses to a standstill.

Gauntlet opened the door of the Chaise.

Athina stepped out, and as an Ostler came hurrying towards them, she said:

"We have need of a Blacksmith, as we have had an accident to a wheel. I hope he is here."

"That 'e were, few minutes ago," the Ostler replied.

"Please fetch him quickly," Athina said.

The Ostler hurried off, and she smiled at Gauntlet.

Then she walked towards the entrance of the Inn.

The Proprietor was standing inside the low-ceilinged hall.

Having appraised the newcomer, he bowed politely.

"Can I help ye, Ma'am?" he asked.

"I have had an accident to a wheel of my Chaise," Athina replied. "I am hoping your Blacksmith can mend it, but as it is getting late, I must stay the night."

"I'll be able to accommodate ye, Ma'am," the Proprietor replied.

"I would like your best bedroom," Athina said. "My luggage is at the back of the Chaise, and I also require a room for my groom."

"That'll be seen to immediately," the Proprietor promised.

He sent a Porter scurrying to collect Athina's luggage.

Then an elderly housemaid in a mob-cap was called to show her upstairs.

The stairs were of oak and uncarpeted, but well polished.

The bedroom into which Athina was shown was comfortable, though, of course, not luxurious.

It was on the First Floor, which indicated to Athina that there was nothing better.

She told the maid it would suit her and she would be staying for only one night.

"Are you busy at the moment?" Athina asked conversationally as they waited for the Porter to bring up the luggage.

"Us've a number o' gent'men stayin' on their way from th' races, Ma'am," the maid replied, "but otherwoise things be a bit dull."

The Porter brought in Athina's small trunk which was all she had required for one night with her Aunt.

As the maid started to unpack, she took off her hat, which was somewhat dusty, and changed her gown.

By the time she had washed, it was dark outside.

She knew, as there was no moon, that it would have been impossible to drive home through the narrow lanes.

"I am far safer here," she told herself, "for we might have had a serious accident if we had continued."

At the same time, she knew that Mrs. Beckwith was expecting her.

She would be worried when she did not arrive as she had said she would.

"We will leave directly after breakfast," she decided, "and will be home well before luncheon."

She told the maid to call her at eight o'clock, thanked her for helping her with her gown, then went downstairs.

The Dining-Room was large and had a beamed ceiling like the hall.

There was a fire burning in the grate.

It had been a cold Spring and, although the days were beginning to be warm, it was still chilly at night.

The Proprietor was at the foot of the stairs as Athina descended, and he waited for her.

"I've kept a table for ye, Ma'am," he said, " 'tis close to the fire, an' I hopes ye'll enjoy yer dinner."

"I am sure I shall," Athina answered.

She had remembered, when the maid was not looking, to slip a ring onto the third finger of her left hand.

It was a pretty ring with three diamonds and had belonged to her Mother.

By twisting it round so that the diamonds were on the inside of her hand, it looked like a wedding-ring.

The Proprietor escorted her to the table he had described.

Athina was pleased to find that she was on her own.

The rest of the tables at the other end of the room were occupied.

When she had ordered what she wanted to eat, the Proprietor hurried away to the kitchen.

She was then able to look at her fellow-guests.

At one table there were three elegantly dressed young men.

They were laughing somewhat loudly while apparently celebrating or anticipating a win at the races.

At two other tables there were what Athina thought must be Commercial Travellers.

Then there was an elderly couple.

The woman had a shawl over her shoulders and she guessed they were staying in the Inn and were not just travellers.

She started to make up stories about each of the guests.

Then at the other side of the fireplace she saw there was a man who was obviously a Gentleman.

With him was a small boy.

She had not noticed them at first, but was made aware of their presence when she heard the Gentleman speaking sharply to the waiter.

He had apparently brought him a bottle of wine different from what he had ordered.

The Gentleman cursed him for being stupid.

Looking at the Gentleman without appearing to

do so, Athina thought he looked disagreeable and bad-tempered.

She suspected he was also a heavy drinker.

The little boy with him was obviously very young, she guessed about six years of age.

He had fair hair and looked a rather delicate child.

Athina thought he also looked very tired.

She wondered where they were going and what their relationship was.

Her dinner arrived and she started to eat.

As she did so, she heard the Gentleman complaining about the food and sending away one dish because the meat was cut too thickly.

She thought, whoever he was, her Father would have disapproved of him.

"I dislike men who shout at waiters," he had said once.

He himself had never shouted at his servants.

If he rebuked them, it was in a cool, quiet manner which was far more effective than if he had raged at them.

The Gentleman, who obviously had ordered a large meal, was still complaining as Athina finished hers.

She felt that while the food admittedly was not very exciting, it was edible, and, on the whole, well cooked.

She had also been attended to without there being any long waits.

When she thanked the waiter, he said:

"It's bin a pleasure waitin' on ye, Ma'am."

She smiled and left the Dining-Room.

She could still hear the Gentleman's voice by the time she reached the foot of the stairs.

A Porter hurried to stop her before she went any farther.

"Yer groom, Ma'am," he said, "told me t' tell ye tha' th' wheels of yer Chaise 'as been repaired."

"Thank you," Athina replied.

Once in her bedroom, she undressed and found she was unexpectedly tired.

Listening to her Aunt saying over and over again the same things which she had heard so often before was always exhausting.

They had also come quite a long distance to where they were now.

"I should sleep well," Athina told herself.

She said her prayers, and as she said them she thought, as she always did, that her Father was near her.

Also her Mother, whom she had adored and who had died two years previously.

They had both been, she recalled, charming and delightful people.

The sad thing was that they did not get on and did not even like each other.

It had taken Athina some years before she had realised how divided her parents were.

It was all due to the fact that theirs, as with most aristocrats, had been an arranged marriage.

When she was old enough to talk to her Mother intelligently, the Countess had confided in her.

When she was young she had fallen very much

in love with the son of the neighbouring Squire.

"We had known each other since we were children," the Countess said. "Then, when I was seventeen and he was twenty-one we realised that we were in love."

"How romantic, Mama!" Athina had said. "What did you do about it?"

"We used to meet secretly," the Countess said, "as William did not wish to approach my Father until he had finished his time at Oxford and had seen a little of the world."

"So he went abroad, Mama."

"Only for a short time," the Countess said. "When he came back, we knew that we were more in love with each other than we had been before. William then said he would talk to my Father."

There was a note in the Countess's voice as she said this that made Athina ask:

"What happened?"

"It had all been arranged that I should go to London that Spring to be presented at Court and to have a Season in which I was to enjoy the Balls. William asked me if I wished to wait until after I had been presented before he asked Papa if we could be engaged. I very stupidly said that perhaps I should be presented first."

She sighed before she went on:

"I thought it would make me seem more grown-up and more capable of knowing my own mind."

"Then you suspected that your Father would not really welcome William as a son-in-law," Athina said.

"I was sure my Father would want me to make an important marriage."

"Because you were so beautiful!" Athina finished.

Her mother smiled.

"I think that was the reason, and also my Father was an ambitious man who had somehow failed to become of any importance himself."

"So what happened?" Athina asked.

"Foolishly I went to London. I was presented at Buckingham Palace, and while I was there your Father saw me. . . ."

Now there was a note in her Mother's voice which Athina could not help knowing was one of despair.

"And Papa fell in love with you," she murmured.

"He wanted to marry me," her Mother said, "mainly because he needed a young wife who would give him a son."

Athina just stared at her Mother, thinking this was something she had never realised before.

"He talked to my Father and Mother," the Countess went on, "and of course they were over-joyed that I should marry anyone so important as the Earl of Murling. They had never aspired so high, even though I was thought to be very pretty."

"And what happened to William?" Athina asked.

Her mother made a helpless gesture. "I had to say good-bye to him, and it broke his heart as it broke mine."

"Was there nothing you could do to persuade your Father that you loved him?"

"I tried to tell him that," the Countess said, "but he would not listen to me. Everybody thought I was the luckiest girl in the world to have captured an Earl before I was even launched onto the Social World! So we were married."

Her Mother did not say any more.

Athina, however, knew that she had never loved the man she had been forced to marry.

What is more, he had been disappointed in her.

It might have been Fate, or it might have simply been because she was unhappy, that the Countess had produced only one child, and that was a daughter.

The Doctors had said they thought it was impossible for her to bear any more children.

At first the Earl would not listen to them, saying that he had never heard such nonsense.

His wife was young and beautiful and it was only a question of time.

But the longed-for son did not arrive.

He was therefore forced to accept the fact that Athina would be his only child.

He was determined to make her exceptional.

It was his way of hiding the truth, that he was bitterly disappointed that the son he wanted so desperately would never materialise.

Loving both her parents, Athina found it hard not to be aware every day and every hour how much they resented each other.

She would talk animatedly and excitedly to her Father.

But when her Mother came into the room, it seemed suddenly as if the temperature had dropped.

There was a restriction over whatever they said that she could not ignore.

Then Athina's Mother had died one very cold Winter when she contracted pneumonia.

It passed through Athina's mind that perhaps her Father would marry again, but he was too old.

Over sixty, he had made the best of his life by making his daughter his companion instead of the son he craved for.

He therefore carried on, Athina thought, with some relief, without a wife with whom he had always felt frustrated.

When he had taken a fall out hunting, the Doctors had said it was nothing serious.

But he died a week later.

It seemed unbelievable to Athina that she should suddenly find herself all alone.

The one thing she had learnt from her parents' marriage was that never in any circumstances would she marry a man she did not love.

"Never, never," she told herself, "will I live like Papa and Mama—both so charming in themselves and both so unhappy because apart from me they had nothing in common."

She was not certain what sort of man she wanted.

But one thing she did know—she would never allow anybody, whoever they might be, to choose her husband for her.

Almost as soon as the Funeral was over, that was exactly what her relations had wanted to do.

They swept into the house, one after another.

The conversation was always the same.

"You cannot live alone, Athina Dear, and the sooner we find you a suitable husband, the better!"

"I have no wish to be married," Athina answered firmly.

"That is ridiculous" would be the answer. "You are already eighteen, and if you are not careful, you will be 'on the shelf.' "

They would laugh at the idea, but Athina knew it was what they thought was the truth.

"You will meet plenty of men in London," one relative after another said.

Even before she had finished her last months of mourning, they began to bring men into the house to meet her.

"Lord Newcomb is staying with us for only two days," an Aunt would say, "and it seems a pity, as he is here in the country, for you not to meet him."

Or else the excuse might be:

"I know Sir Willoughby would be thrilled to see your Father's horses. Take him round the stable, Athina Dear, while I sit in front of the fire."

As soon as they arrived, Athina felt that every nerve was on edge.

Her whole body rebelled at the thought that the newcomer was there for one reason only, to look her over as if she were on show at a Spring Fair.

"No! No! No!" she wanted to scream. "Go away and leave me alone. I do not want to marry you, or anybody else."

However, one of the many things her Father had taught her was self-control.

She was charming and polite.

No-one had the slightest idea what she was feeling inside.

One man, more importunate than the rest, returned unexpectedly and alone the next day.

When he had actually proposed to her, she said what was in her mind.

"I am, of course, honoured, My Lord," she said in a cold voice, "that after such a short acquaintance you should ask me to be your wife, but I must make it clear that I have no intention of marrying anyone."

"That is ridiculous!" he had replied. "Of course you will have to be married. No woman should live alone, and certainly no-one as beautiful as you."

"I have plenty of people to look after me," Athina said, "and although you may think it strange, I like being alone with, of course, my horses, my friends, and my Estate."

She saw a look in his eyes which told her that her Estate was as desirable to him as she was herself.

In fact, without it, it was doubtful if he would have been so eager.

She held out her hand.

"Good-bye, My Lord, and thank you for calling, but I think you will understand when I tell you it would be a mistake for you to come again."

There was nothing her Suitor could do but leave.

She told herself with a little smile it was "with his tail between his legs."

Athina stretched herself out on the goose-feather mattress which was very comfortable and shut her eyes.

Tomorrow, she thought, she would be home, and that was where she wanted to be.

It was then, as she was just falling asleep, that she heard a scream.

chapter two

IT was the high scream of something small that was frightened.

As Athina listened, she heard a harsh voice say:

"I have been waiting for you! Where the devil have you been?"

It was easy to recognise the voice of the Gentleman who had dined opposite her and who had been so offensive to the waiters.

He was speaking to the little boy who had been with him, and she heard the boy reply:

"I . . . went to . . . the stables. I thought . . . *Ladybird* was . . . unhappy because you . . . whipped her."

"It has nothing to do with you whether I whip my horses or not," the Gentleman said angrily, "and you will not go out of the Inn unless I tell you to. It is time you learnt how to behave yourself."

He must have made a threatening gesture, for the boy cried out.

"Please . . . I am . . . sorry. Do not . . . beat me . . . again!"

"I am going to teach you to obey me!" the Gentleman thundered.

There was another scream, and Athina thought the child must be trying to escape.

There was a noise as if two people were scuffling.

Then there was a thud as if the boy had been thrown onto the bed.

He was screaming again, screaming so that it was unbearable to hear him.

With hands that trembled, she relit the candle she had blown out.

When there was light in the room, she realised why she was hearing what was happening so clearly.

It was because there was a communicating-door between her and the boy's bedroom.

She had not noticed it before.

The screams were gradually growing weaker, and now the child was mumbling and she thought he was saying:

"Mum-ma! Mum-ma!"

"That will teach you not to disobey me again," the Gentleman said in the same aggressive voice. "I will beat obedience into you if it is the last thing I do!"

Athina heard him walk across the room and open the door to slam it shut behind him.

She also thought she heard him turn the key in the lock.

She got out of bed and, putting on her dressing-gown, went to the communicating-door.

Now the boy was just sobbing piteously as if he had not the strength to make any loud sound.

She knew she had to help him.

She looked at the door and saw there was a key on her side of it.

She turned it in the lock, then opened the door cautiously.

She did this just in case she had been mistaken and the Gentleman was still there.

By the light of two candles she could see the room was much smaller than hers.

There was just a single bed on which the boy was lying face down.

His coat must have been pulled off him, because it was lying in a heap on the floor.

He was wearing only his shirt and trousers.

She went into the room.

As she drew nearer to him, she could see blood from the weals on his back beginning to stain the whiteness of his shirt.

He was sobbing convulsively, while at the same time murmuring: "Mum-ma! Mum-ma!" in a broken little voice.

She sat down on the bed and put her hand very gently on his fair head.

"It is all right," she said in a soft voice. "It is all over now, and he will not hurt you any more."

For a moment the boy was still.

Then he raised himself as if to look at her, but his eyes were swollen and blinded by his tears.

"It is all right," Athina said again. "I will not let him hurt you any more."

It was then the small boy flung himself against her.

He clung to her, saying: "Mum-ma! Mum-ma!" as if he thought she was his mother.

She wanted to take him in her arms, but was afraid of hurting his back.

Instead, she held him by his shoulders and continued to say quietly:

"It is all right. It is all over."

It was some time before his tears ceased.

When they did, she said:

"Now, come into my room and I will put something on your back which will take away the pain."

The boy held on to her for a moment as if he were afraid she was going to leave him.

Then, as she rose to her feet, she helped him to the ground.

His small face was wet with tears, and she had to guide him round the bed and out of the room into hers.

Only when she had shut the door and locked it did she say in a normal tone of voice:

"No-one can hear us now, and I am going to make you feel very much better than you do at the moment."

She made him sit down on her bed.

She brought back a sponge and a linen towel from the wash-hand-stand.

Gently she washed his face, holding the sponge against his eyes to cool them.

He sat still while she did so and while she dried his face with the towel.

Now that she could see him clearly, she realised that he was a very attractive little boy.

There was no doubt that he was suffering from shock and was, she thought, not quite certain what was happening.

"I am going to put some cream on your back," she said quietly, "so take off your shirt."

He fumbled with the buttons and in the end she had to help him.

When she took the shirt away, she gave a gasp of horror.

His whole back was covered with weals from the whip the Gentleman had used on him.

She could see there were many other weals from previous whippings.

She thought it would be a mistake to try to make him give her an explanation.

She went to the dressing-table.

She came back with the cream she used on her face when her skin was dry from the Winter winds.

She used it when she had been out hunting or when, like today, she had been covered with dust.

She turned the small boy round a little so that she could sit behind him.

"I will try not to hurt you," she said, "but this cream will soon heal your skin. In the meantime, it will stop the weals from hurting you."

She applied it very carefully, more horrified every moment as she realised how often the child had been beaten.

Then, without telling him what she was doing, she went back next door to fetch his nightshirt.

She had noticed it, when she had gone into his room, lying at the end of the bed.

She slipped it over his head.

Then she said:

"You will be much more comfortable now, and if you go to sleep, you will feel better in the morning."

As she spoke, she realised that the little boy was looking at her as if he were seeing her for the first time.

"I want my Mum-ma!" he said. "But she has gone away and will . . . never come . . . back."

She could hardly hear what he said.

The pain in his voice and in his eyes was unmistakable.

"Your Mother is dead?" Athina said.

The boy nodded.

He was looking at her like a small animal who did not understand what was happening to him.

She knew he was thinking he did not want to leave her.

"I will tell you what we will do," she said. "If you take off your trousers, you can get into bed and tell me about your Mother."

As if it were an order, he got to his feet and slipped off his trousers beneath his nightshirt.

Rather gingerly, because his back was obviously hurting him, he got into her bed.

It was a large one, and there was plenty of room for Athina to get in on the other side.

She put her head down on the pillow, and as if he knew she expected him to do the same, he lay down, facing her.

"Now," she said, "we can talk without being overheard. First you must tell me what your name is."

"It is Peter—Peter Naver," he said.

"And who is the man who is being so unkind to you?"

There was a little pause before Peter answered:

"He is—my Stepfather. Mum-ma married him . . . after Papa was . . . killed."

"And you live with him?" Athina asked.

"Yes—he is my—Guardian."

Athina knew that Guardians had complete control over their Wards.

At the same time, it seemed strange that a Stepfather should want to keep the child of his dead wife.

"Have you no other relations?" she asked.

"We have . . . been to see my . . . Grandmother . . . today," Peter answered, "and she . . . asked me to . . . stay with her, but Step-Papa would . . . not let me."

"Why not?" Athina asked.

Peter made a helpless little gesture with his hands.

She was aware that he had no answer to that question.

"What was your Mother's name before she married your Papa?" she enquired.

Peter could answer this.

"She was . . . Lady Louise Rock," he said, "and . . . I miss her. I wish I . . . could . . . die and be . . . with her."

31

He was crying again.

Instinctively Athina reached out and drew him nearer to her.

He put his head against her shoulder.

"I want my Mum-ma," he said. "I want . . . to be . . . with . . . her."

"I know you do," Athina said, "but she is near you even though you cannot see her, and she is very upset to think you are so unhappy."

Peter stopped crying.

"She is near me? Really—near me?" he asked. "Like the . . . Angels?"

"Yes, just like that," Athina said as she smiled, "and I expect your Mother once told you that you had an Angel watching over you, and now she is looking after you too."

"Are you—sure? Quite . . . sure?" Peter asked.

"Of course I am," Athina replied.

"Then why does . . . she let . . . Step-Papa be so . . . cruel to me? He . . . beats me and . . . beats me . . . nothing I . . . do is . . . right."

"That is something we must prevent happening ever again," Athina said.

She thought Peter was thinking this over, and went on:

"I want to help you, Peter, and I think it was your Mother who brought me here tonight so that I could learn how cruelly your Stepfather is treating you and take you away from him."

As she spoke, it was as if somebody else were putting the words into her mouth.

It struck her that although it was a strange thing to say, she had to say it.

"You will—take me . . . away from . . . Step-Papa?" Peter asked eagerly.

"I will certainly do my best," Athina answered, "but you will have to tell me a little more about your Mother. You say her name was Lady Louise Rock?"

"Yes . . . that is . . . right," Peter confirmed. "She lived in a big house which was . . . also called 'Rock,' and I always thought it was a . . . funny name for a . . . house."

Athina gave an exclamation.

"Are you telling me," she asked, "that your Mother was the daughter of the Marquess of Rockingdale?"

Peter nodded.

"She used to . . . tell me about . . . my Grand-father, who was a . . . very important man. His house . . . which is called 'Rock' is very . . . very . . . big."

Athina found it hard to believe.

She knew Rock Park; of course she did.

It was very near where she herself lived.

She had never been there, although her parents had.

The Marquess of Rockingdale had died two or three years ago.

Her Father had then said that he had no use for the son who had succeeded to the title.

"He spends all his time in London," he said to Athina, "with a lot of beautiful women instead of

33

attending to his Estate. I have no time for those young toffs who think they are the 'Smart Set'!"

Athina had however hoped that when she was grown up she would be invited to Rock Park.

She wanted to see the inside of it.

Her Father and Mother had described it to her, and it was actually one of the sights of the County.

The Estate was large, and at one point bordered with her Father's.

She had hunted over some of it, but that was only by accident.

The last Marquess, because he had grown so old, did not ride to hounds.

The present one preferred to hunt in Leicestershire, where he had a Hunting-Lodge.

Nevertheless, what was important at the moment was that he was the Uncle of this defenceless little boy.

He would have to do something about the way he was being treated.

"When did your Mother leave you?" she asked gently.

"A long time ago," Peter replied, "when I was just six and now I am nearly . . . seven."

'Almost a year of this Devil torturing him,' Athina thought.

It seemed strange that none of the Family knew what was happening.

Peter was still cuddling against her, and she asked:

"Why did you not tell your Grandmama when

she asked you to stay with her that you were un-happy with your Stepfather?"

"I wanted to," Peter said, "but Step-Papa was in the room and he . . . gripped my arm and . . . said: 'Peter wants to stay with me, do you not, Peter?' "

Peter drew in his breath.

"I could . . . not say 'no' because he was . . . pinching my arm . . . pinching it so . . . hard that it . . . hurt."

Athina thought the more she heard about Peter's Stepfather, the more she loathed him.

Now she asked somewhat belatedly:

"You have not told me your Stepfather's name."

"He is . . . Lord B-Burnham of A-Avon," Peter said, faltering a little over the words. "He is very . . . important in the House of Lords and . . . everybody is . . . frightened of . . . him."

There was silence for a moment.

Then he said, as if he were talking to himself:

"I am . . . frightened and his . . . horses are . . . frightened. *Ladybird* is . . . unhappy tonight. I know . . . she is . . . unhappy."

"Which is why you went to see her," Athina said softly. "That was very brave and kind of you."

"I love *Ladybird* and I love . . . all Step-Papa's . . . horses, and when he . . . whips them I . . . know what . . . they are . . . feeling."

He made a little movement as he spoke, as if his back hurt him.

Athina knew she had heard enough.

She was absolutely determined that Lord Burn-ham would no longer be able to terrorise his Step-son.

Very gently she put Peter's head down on the pillow beside her.

"Now go to sleep," she said. "In the morning we are going to do something very exciting and I do not want you to be tired."

"I am tired . . . now," Peter said. "It was a . . . long drive. We went a . . . very long . . . way and the . . . dust made my throat . . . dry, but . . . Step-Papa would . . . not let me . . . have any . . . water."

Athina felt that if she heard any more about Lord Burnham, she would murder him with her own hands.

She knew she would have to be clever if she was to save Peter.

She kissed his cheek and he put his arms round her neck.

"You are like Mum-ma," he said, "just like my Mum-ma."

"Then go to sleep and dream of her," Athina answered, "and remember that she is here beside you, looking after you, and she has told me to help you escape."

"From . . . Step-Papa?"

"From your Step-Papa," Athina confirmed.

It was a vow rather than a promise.

After all the small boy had been through, he was so exhausted that he fell asleep almost immediately.

Athina blew out the candle, then lay planning what she should do.

She realised it would be difficult to get Peter away from the Inn without having a scene with Lord Burnham.

She therefore willed herself to wake at five

o'clock, when she knew the maids would be stirring.

Her Father had been in the Army.

He had taught her how to wake, as he could, at whatever hour she pleased.

"It is just a question of will-power," he said, "and telling your subconscious to carry out your wishes so that there is no need for reveille or alarms of any sort."

Athina at the age of twelve had found it a challenge.

Soon she could wake, as her Father could, at any time she desired.

Now she forced herself to relax.

She had already planned in her mind that she would get Peter away from the Inn without Lord Burnham being aware of it.

She also said a very special prayer not only to God, but also to Lady Louise, that she would be successful.

"I have to save your little son from that brute," she said, "but you will have to help me. It may not be easy, but I am sure when your brother knows what is happening, he will take action."

She only hoped she was right.

As if Lady Louise answered her prayer, she fell asleep.

Neither she nor Peter moved until it was five o'clock.

*　*　*

Athina awoke, and for a moment could not remember where she was.

Then she saw the small fair head on the pillow next to hers and remembered what had happened last night.

She got out of bed quietly so as not to disturb Peter, and opened the door onto the corridor.

As she expected, she could hear movements down below.

The maids were already cleaning the Entrance Hall and the Dining-Room.

She waited until one of them passed by at the bottom of the stairs, then, raising her voice, she called:

"Good-morning!"

The maid looked up and saw her.

"I am Mrs. Beckwith," Athina said. "Would you be so kind as to tell my groom that I wish to have my Chaise round in half-an-hour?"

"Oi' tell 'im, Ma'am," the maid replied.

Athina went back into her bedroom and started to dress.

She then packed her trunk.

Going into Peter's room, she collected his coat which was still on the floor.

She saw, too, he had a leather bag in which his other things were packed.

She guessed Lord Burnham would have brought his Valet with him, who also attended to Peter.

She knew this could be dangerous, as the man would certainly be up earlier than his Master.

She went back into her own room and locked the communicating-door between their two rooms.

Then she woke Peter, who sat up, rubbing his eyes.

"I was . . . dreaming," he said, "dreaming that Mum-Mum-ma was . . . with me."

Athina kissed him and said:

"She was with you. Now, listen, if we are to escape, you will have to dress quickly, then I will tell you what to do."

"Can I go . . . away with . . . you?" Peter asked.

"That is what you are going to do," Athina answered, "but hurry!"

He jumped out of bed and started to put on his clothes.

He did it so quickly that Athina knew he was used to dressing himself.

All she had to do was to tie the laces of his shoes.

By this time it was after half-past-five.

She knew that if Gauntlet had received her message, he would be already in the court-yard.

The vital thing was that Peter should go through the hall and into the yard without being questioned.

"Now, listen, Peter," she said, "I want you to go downstairs, just as you did last night when you went out to see *Ladybird*."

"Am I to . . . see her . . . now?"

"No, you must not do that," Athina said, "because your Stepfather's groom or his Valet might see you."

Peter seemed to understand, and she went on:

"Go out through the door into the yard, and

when you get there, hurry as quickly as you can towards the gate."

"The gate by which we . . . came in?"

"Yes, that is the one I mean. Then turn right—do you know which is right?"

Peter held out his hand to prove that he did.

"Good! Then go right and walk along the road, but do not run. Just walk and I will join you in the Chaise as quickly as I can."

"Then I . . . will get . . . in with . . . you?" Peter asked.

"That is the idea," Athina answered. "Do not talk to anybody. Just do exactly as I have told you. It is important that nobody should notice you."

"No-one . . . noticed me . . . last night," Peter said.

"But then it was dark," Athina reminded him, "and although it is very early in the morning, people may be moving about."

Peter nodded his head as if he understood.

She smiled at him.

"Off you go, then," she said, "and just walk along the road."

She let him out through the door.

She waited until she thought he would be outside the Inn before she went downstairs.

A Porter in his shirt-sleeves was clearing away empty beer-mugs.

"Would you be kind enough to bring down the two pieces of luggage which are upstairs in my bedroom?" Athina asked him.

He looked up in surprise because she was so early.

At the same time, because she spoke in a tone of authority, he replied: "Yes, Ma'am," and went up the stairs.

Athina went up to the desk and was glad to see that there was no sign of the Proprietor.

There was, however, another Porter who appeared to be in charge.

She asked him what she owed and paid the bill, leaving a tip for the staff.

He thanked her and she hurried through the door and into the yard.

With a sense of relief she saw Gauntlet waiting with the horses between the shafts.

"Good-morning, Gauntlet!" she said. "I was afraid you might not have got my message."

" 'Marnin', Ma'am. I were surprised Your Ladyship wantin' t'leave so early!" Gauntlet replied.

Athina did not answer.

She was busy getting into the riding-seat and picking up the reins.

As she did so, the Porter who had gone to fetch her luggage came out of the Inn.

He was carrying her small trunk and Peter's leather bag.

Quickly, before Gauntlet could question the strange leather bag, she said to him:

"That is my bag too. Put them both in!"

Gauntlet did as he was told, and Athina handed him a half-sovereign to give to the Porter.

It was a large tip, but she hoped that if there was a commotion over the disappearance of Peter, he would not want to involve her.

As soon as Gauntlet was beside her, she drove off.

She turned the horses to the right as they left the entrance to the court-yard.

As she did so, she looked down the road, but could see no sign of Peter.

For a moment she felt her heart stop.

What could have happened?

Had he been apprehended by His Lordship's Valet?

Or had he misunderstood her instructions?

Then, as the horses moved on, she saw him come out of the hedgerow where he must have been hiding.

She gave a sigh of relief.

It told her more forcefully than words how much the small boy already meant to her.

She had known last night that she would have done anything—anything to save him from the bestial cruelty of Lord Burnham.

Although it seemed incredible, she was sure she was being directed.

Guided by a Power that was not of this world.

To Gauntlet sitting beside her she said:

"We are not going straight home, but to Rock Park."

Gauntlet did not seem very surprised. He only replied:

"There be two grooms at th' Inn who'd been at th' Races. They'd made a bet on 'Is Lordship's horse."

Athina thought they must have been in the employment of the young man in the Dining-Room.

They also had doubtless backed the winner.

As she drove on, Gauntlet said as if he were speaking to himself:

" 'Is Lordship'll be the next Master of the Horse, now Lord Edward Rock be dead."

Athina had read of Lord Edward's death in *The Times*.

She had not been particularly interested, although her Father had known him.

Now she said:

"You see that small boy just ahead. He is coming with us to Rock Park."

She thought Gauntlet would ask questions.

But he merely nodded and replied:

"Very good, M'Lady, an' Rock Park be on our way 'ome."

"I know that," Athina answered.

She pulled the horses to a standstill beside Peter and he climbed into the Chaise.

"We have . . . done it! We have done . . . it!" he cried excitedly.

Without saying anything, Gauntlet moved into a seat behind and Peter sat beside Athina.

He moved close to her and put his cheek on her arm.

"I was . . . frightened," he said, "in case . . . you did not . . . come, or Step-Papa . . . stopped . . . you."

"Did you see anybody you recognised as you went through the court-yard?" Athina asked.

Peter shook his head.

"I hurried, as you told me, and there was nobody

about except the man who was with these horses."

"That is Gauntlet, and he is my groom," Athina explained. "It was clever of you to get away without being seen."

"Step-Papa will be very ... very ... angry when he ... finds me ... gone!" Peter murmured.

"I know that," Athina answered.

"He ... will ... beat me ... again."

"He will have to find you first," Athina replied, "and I will tell you where we are going. We are going to Rock Park to see your Uncle who, as I expect you know, is the Marquess of Rockingdale."

"Will he ... stop Step-Papa from ... beating me?" Peter asked.

"I know he will," Athina answered.

As she spoke, she thought that whatever the Marquess was like, he could not allow the child to be so brutally treated.

"Lord Burnham is a beast!" she told herself. "If the Marquess has any 'guts,' as my Father would say, he will tell him so!"

Peter made himself comfortable.

At the same time, he was still sitting very close to her.

It was as if he felt she protected him and there was no chance of his being snatched away unexpectedly.

Because Athina could feel his fear vibrating from him, she drove faster than she would have done otherwise.

Once again they had to turn off into the narrow

lane where they had clashed with the farm-wagon the previous night.

She was careful, but she was now in a greater hurry than she had been the night before.

Every minute that passed brought them nearer to the time when Peter's absence would be discovered.

Lord Burnham would either send his Valet or go himself to the boy's bedroom, and find it empty.

He had locked the door into the corridor, so he would quickly realise that Peter must have left through the communicating-door.

To make things more difficult, Athina had locked that door on her side.

She then put the key in one of the drawers of the dressing-table.

At least there would be a further delay until the key was found.

She also guessed that Lord Burnham, however determined he was to search for his Stepson, would not leave the Inn without first having breakfast.

Athina was sure Lord Burnham was a very astute man.

Therefore, when he was convinced that Peter was not in the Inn or the stables, he would know that somebody had helped him to escape.

He would learn from the servants that she and Gauntlet had left the Inn very early.

He would learn that she had occupied the adjacent room.

There was, therefore, every likelihood that Peter had gone away with her.

It would certainly seem more likely than that Peter had gone with the race-goers, the Commercial Travellers, or anyone else who was staying in the Inn last night.

It took Athina nearly two hours before she could turn in at the high and impressive wrought-iron gold-tipped gates of Rock Park.

As she went up the drive lined with ancient oak trees, she found herself praying that the Marquess would be there.

Also that he would understand and hopefully thank her for bringing Peter away from the man who was treating him so abominably.

"How can he be anything but grateful?" she asked herself.

At the same time, remembering the stories she had heard of the Marquess's reputation, she was not sure.

She looked ahead.

Rock Park was a very magnificent building.

The sunshine seemed suddenly to illuminate the standard on the flagpole above the roof.

It waved slowly in the morning breeze.

The fact that it was flying meant that the Marquess was in residence.

Athina's heart gave a leap.

She was sure it was a good omen.

chapter three

THE Marquess of Rockingdale drove his Dog-cart
down Piccadilly.

He was not surprised that people looked at him
in admiration.

He had just received it from his Coach-builders,
and it was in fact partly his own design.

The Dog-cart had become fashionable and was
modelled on the Phaeton which had been in use
among the Bucks and Beaux of the Regency.

The wheels were reduced in size and the body
itself was not so high.

The new look had delighted the Country Squires.

This was because their dogs could run beneath
it, which protected them from being endangered
by other traffic.

The Marquess had trained two highly bred Dalmatians to run under a Dog-cart he already had.

With the new one there would be more room for
the dogs.

Painted black with yellow wheels and uphol-
stery, the Dog-cart was striking in itself.

It was even more striking, however, when it was drawn by *Samson*.

This was a jet black horse which had already won a number of prizes.

What the Marquess did not realise was that he himself was even more striking than his conveyance.

He wore a shining black top-hat on one side of his dark head and a yellow waist-coat which matched the vehicle.

He attracted the attention of every woman he passed.

At the same time, every man looked enviously at his horse.

It was a sunny day and the ladies on their way to Rotten Row were riding in open Victorias.

They were holding tiny lace-trimmed sunshades over their elaborate hats.

One after another they waved at the Marquess.

He had hardly replaced his hat before he had to raise it again.

He noticed the Countess of Gaythorne, with whom he had had an ardent *affaire de coeur* the year before.

He retained a certain affection for her, although he had left her.

This was because she had been too demonstrative in public.

One thing the Marquess disliked was parading his feelings.

It gave the gossips even more to talk about than they had already.

It was not surprising that they talked about him.

He was not only extremely handsome, but the owner of a title that was part of English history.

He was also immensely rich.

Apart from this, he had an intelligent mind and could on occasions be exceedingly witty.

Men liked him even though they were jealous, not only of his possessions, but also of his achievements.

He was an outstanding rider, a first-class Polo player, and excelled at every sport in which he was interested.

Travelling a little farther along the road, the Marquess passed the Countess of Stretton.

She had been acclaimed as one of the great Beauties of the century.

She nodded her head to him, but there was a coolness in the look she gave him.

This was because he had not yet succumbed to her attractions.

Almost every other man in the Social World was ready to be at her beck and call.

So far, however, the Marquess had eluded her.

There was something fastidious in his make up which told him that he did not wish to be one of a queue.

If other men pursued any particular woman, it was typical of the Marquess to turn in the opposite direction.

The truth was, he told himself, that he wanted something unique.

Then he laughed because it was a very difficult

thing to find in the Social Set in which he moved.

In fact, if a woman was beautiful, it was inevitable that the Prince of Wales was there first.

After that, there would be a scramble amongst the smart young men.

They, like the Marquess, were always looking for somebody to amuse them.

The Marquess was at the moment, however, not thinking of women, but of the interview he was about to have with the Lord Chamberlain.

He had waited, he thought, for a long time.

Now what he most desired was within his grasp.

It was traditional for the Head of the Rockingdale Family to be the Master of the Horse.

The Earls of Rockingdale had held that position under George III and George IV.

It was at the end of the latter reign that the Earldom was made into a Marquessate.

The first Marquess of Rockingdale was therefore Master of the Horse to William IV and the young Queen Victoria.

Unfortunately, he died in an accident when he was not yet fifty, and the present Marquess's Father refused the position.

He said he had no wish to spend his time at Court.

He hoped, however, his son would have different ideas.

But his son was at the time only a small boy and the position was instead given to his Uncle, Lord Edward Rock.

He performed his duties reasonably well.

At the same time, he did not have many horses himself, and was not an outstanding owner as his predecessors had been.

Now the young Marquess had succeeded his Father, and Lord Edward having died, he looked forward with pleasure to taking his place.

He had already thought of many improvements he would make to the Royal Stables.

He was making a formal call on the Earl of Latham, who was the Lord Chamberlain.

His office was in St. James's Palace, where he dealt with all the details connected with Court Ceremonial.

The Marquess drove down St. James's Street.

He was aware that the members of White's who were going in and out of the Club were looking at him.

Some he knew must be curious as to where he was going.

He reached St. James's Palace and drew up his horse outside the main door.

When he stepped down, his place was taken by his groom.

He had been sitting behind with his arms folded in the correct manner.

He wore the Rockingdale livery and a cockaded top-hat.

The Marquess walked into the Palace.

There was no need for anybody to guide him to the Lord Chamberlain's Office.

He had been there frequently and the Earl of Latham was a man he both respected and liked.

As he appeared, the Earl rose from the chair in which he was sitting and held out his hand.

He was a tall, handsome man whose hair and beard were just beginning to turn white.

He cut a distinguished figure at the Drawing-Rooms and every State occasion.

"Good-morning, Denzil," he said as the Marquess appeared. "I was expecting you."

"I thought you would be, My Lord," the Marquess replied.

"I hear you had a winner two days ago," the Earl said, "but that is nothing unusual."

The Marquess smiled and sat down in a chair in front of the Lord Chamberlain's desk.

"You know, of course, why I have called to see you," the Marquess said. "I need not tell you that I am impatient to take up the position of Master of the Horse."

He paused a moment before he continued:

"I wish to implement the improvements and alterations which I have discussed with you on various occasions."

The Lord Chamberlain did not immediately reply.

The Marquess looked at him enquiringly before finally he said slowly:

"I am afraid, Denzil, I have something to tell you."

The Marquess raised his eye-brows.

"To tell me?" he questioned sharply.

"I know you are expecting to be appointed Master of the Horse, as your forebears were," the Earl continued.

"That is why I am here," the Marquess answered. "But are you telling me that Her Majesty wishes to appoint somebody else?"

There was a note in his voice as if he assumed that the Earl would immediately "pooh-pooh" such a suggestion.

Instead, he said in a somewhat embarrassed manner:

"It is not quite as bad as that."

"Then what is it?" the Marquess asked. "Surely Her Majesty is aware that while it was wrong of my Father to refuse the Office when it was offered to him, I think it is something he later regretted."

He sighed before he went on:

"He was, as you know, not well at the time, having injured his back in a fall out hunting. He felt the responsibility would be too much for him. So it passed to his brother, who was not what you would call an outstanding horseman."

"I am aware of that," the Lord Chamberlain replied, "and Her Majesty appreciates that you have every right to feel the position should be yours. She will in fact confirm the appointment to you, but on one condition."

"Condition?" the Marquess exclaimed. "What can you possibly mean by that?"

Again the Lord Chamberlain paused.

He was very fond of the Marquess, whom he had known since he was a small boy.

Because he was a kindly man, he was finding this a particularly unpleasant interview.

There was again a silence before the Lord Chamberlain said:

"Her Majesty is willing to appoint you as Master of the Horse, but she considers it important that you should first be married or at least engaged."

As he finished speaking, the Marquess stared at the Lord Chamberlain as if he felt that what he had heard could not be true.

"Married?" he said at last. "Why the devil should I be married just to please the Queen?"

Even as he spoke, however, he knew the answer only too well.

What had happened two years ago at Windsor he had hoped by now had been forgotten.

He had been invited to stay for a Ball which was being given for visiting Royalty.

He had not been particularly excited by the invitation, knowing that the protocol at Windsor could be extremely tiresome.

He would far rather be with his friends in London, or at his own house in the country.

However, it was something he could not refuse.

He had accordingly arrived with his Valet, his groom, and a team drawing his carriage.

He knew his horses would be superior to any that would be in the Royal Stables.

The Queen, who liked handsome men, had received him more genially than she had a number of her other guests.

There was the usual audience at which nobody was allowed to sit.

It was followed by a long-drawn-out dinner where everybody spoke in lowered voices.

After that came the Ball, which was a comparatively small one.

The guests danced to what the Marquess considered was an inferior Orchestra.

He was bored, exceedingly bored.

Then he discovered that one of the Queen's Ladies-in-Waiting, who was new, was rather attractive.

Lady Mentmore was the second wife of one of the Gentlemen-at-Arms.

He had married her because he needed an heir.

In consequence, he had chosen somebody young, healthy, and very pretty.

The Marquess danced with her twice more than the Queen would have considered conventional.

He had then suggested that he should say goodnight to her later.

Lady Mentmore shook her head.

"It is too dangerous," she murmured.

" 'Nothing ventured, nothing gained' is my motto," the Marquess replied.

She laughed at him provocatively and he thought again she was very pretty and very desirable.

"Tell me where you are sleeping," he persisted.

"You could never find it," she answered. "We are tucked away, and as the place is like a rabbit-warren, you would get lost and, if you are not careful, might end up in Her Majesty's bedroom!"

They both laughed at the idea.

Finally, the Marquess persuaded Lady Mentmore to meet him on a landing which was situated somewhere between their two rooms.

He would then take her to his.

"You are quite right," he said, "the place is a rabbit-warren and we must take no chances of getting lost."

She was listening to him wide-eyed and he went on:

"I have been told the story a hundred times about the Ambassador who found it impossible to find his own room and slept on a sofa, only to be accused by a chambermaid the next day of having been too drunk to find his way to bed!"

Lady Mentmore had heard the story too, but she giggled attractively.

The Marquess had thought he would definitely enjoy kissing her rose-bud lips.

It seemed a long time before the party ended and the Queen and her guests retired to bed.

The Marquess was installed in the most ancient part of the Castle.

The walls were thick, the passages narrow, where nothing said was likely to be overheard.

At one o'clock in the morning, as arranged, he found his way back to the landing and waited for Lady Mentmore.

He had been there for about five minutes when she appeared.

She was looking very lovely in a silk negligee trimmed with lace.

Her fair hair fell over her shoulders.

There was no need for words.

The Marquess put out his hand to draw her towards him.

Even as he did so, at that very moment a door opened quite near them.

Somebody peeped out and the door was shut quickly again.

Lady Mentmore, who had her back to it, was unaware of what had happened.

But the Marquess, as he guided her to his room, was somewhat perturbed.

He knew only too well how gossip could sweep through the Castle like a North wind.

He had no idea who else was sleeping in that part of the Castle, nor whether it was a man or a woman who had seen him with Lady Mentmore.

Anyway, he told himself philosophically, it was done now.

To send her back to her bedroom would not at all mend matters.

He could only hope that the person who had peeped out was of no consequence.

Lady Mentmore had more than exceeded his expectations.

But the Marquess had thought after that visit that the Queen was slightly more stiff than she had been previously.

There was a disapproving look in her eyes that had not been there before.

Now he understood that he was being punished for what had been a brief, but pleasant, interlude in a dull visit.

He had not been to Windsor Castle again.

He had therefore not come in contact with Lady Mentmore since she had left him in the early hours of the morning.

"I cannot understand, Denzil," the Lord Chamberlain was saying, "what you have done to incur the Queen's displeasure, but as you know only too well, nothing will stop women from gossiping."

That was true.

The Marquess was well aware that quite apart from Lady Mentmore, his reputation was not one which would commend itself to the Queen.

It was certainly no worse than that of her son.

But Her Majesty was known to disapprove of almost everything the Prince of Wales did.

"Does this mean that I have to be married before I can be appointed?"

"Or engaged," the Lord Chamberlain said, "but I think I should warn you that Her Majesty will not leave the position vacant for very long."

"What do you mean by 'very long'?" the Marquess enquired.

"Shall we say two months?" the Lord Chamberlain replied. "That will take you to approximately the middle of June."

He saw the dismay on the Marquess's face and added:

"I am sorry, Denzil. I know this is a blow for you. At the same time, you have to marry sooner or later. Your Father made the mistake of having only two children, and if you take my advice, you will fill what I am sure are the large Nurseries at Rock with a number of them."

The Marquess rose to his feet.

"I loathe the idea of marriage," he said angrily.

"I know that any young, unfledged girl who would have the approval of Her Majesty would bore me to distraction!"

He walked across to the window as he spoke.

There was an expression of compassion in the Lord Chamberlain's eyes as he watched him.

He had been young and dashing himself.

He had enjoyed the favours of a number of women before he married, so he knew exactly what the Marquess was feeling.

"The Season has just started," he said aloud. "There will be many pretty girls coming to London. Some of them have already arrived. If you attend the first Drawing-Room, you will be able to take your pick."

"I would rather choose a horse at Tattersall's or in the Spring Sales," the Marquess snapped. "At least I would not have to be encumbered with it for the rest of my life!"

The Lord Chamberlain sighed.

"You could, of course, refuse the position, as your Father did."

"What excuse could I make?" the Marquess enquired. "At least my Father was a sick man. Even so, there was a huge outcry amongst the Family."

He walked across the room before he went on:

"I have no such excuse, except that I have no wish to be 'leg-shackled' and to choose a wife of whom the Queen would approve."

"She will, of course, be by tradition a Lady-of-the-Bedchamber," the Lord Chamberlain remarked.

"That is exactly what I mean," the Marquess said savagely. "The Queen's choice of a Lady-of-the-Bedchamber is not someone I am likely to find very exciting on the long Winter evenings!"

"Come on now, Denzil, it is not as bad as that!" the Lord Chamberlain said. "After all, young girls, however gauche they may seem when they first appear as *débutantes*, eventually become the polished, sophisticated, exotic women with whom you have been spending your time ever since I can remember."

"But I have not had to marry any of them!" the Marquess said.

As he spoke, he thought that if he were married, he would very much dislike knowing that his wife was having an *affaire de coeur* with somebody like himself.

It was something that had never entered his mind until now.

He had always assumed that his wife would take the place of his Mother as the charming, delightful, chatelaine of Rock.

She would adore him as his Mother had adored his Father to the exclusion of any other man.

He walked back from the window, knowing that the Lord Chamberlain was awaiting his decision, no doubt hoping he would not take too long about it.

Outside, the sun was shining, and the Marquess suddenly thought he must go to the country.

Perhaps at Rock he would be able to think the problem over without being so angry and resentful.

For the moment he felt as if he were being encased between walls.

They were gradually closing in on him and becoming a prison.

"You say I have two months," he said aloud. "Very well, My Lord, you shall have my decision as soon as it is possible to give it to you with, I suppose, the name of the woman I shall marry."

He spoke bitterly, and the Lord Chamberlain said in a quiet voice:

"That, I am afraid, is what Her Majesty will expect."

"I am only surprised," the Marquess said scathingly, "that she does not choose my wife for me and leave me nothing to do except put the ring on her finger!"

"I am sorry, Denzil, very sorry," the Lord Chamberlain said. "If I could have prevented this from happening, I would have, for I knew how much it would upset you."

"It is not your fault," the Marquess said, "but I have always believed it is a mistake to have a woman on the throne rather than a man!"

Because he could not help himself, the Earl laughed.

"Quite a number of people have no doubt thought that at one time or another," he said, "and yet you have to admit that the Queen has made Britain the most powerful country in the world."

He paused a moment and then continued:

"You have only to look at your map to know that

every day the areas coloured red to signify British rule increase and multiply!"

"I know, I know," the Marquess said testily, "but when one is affected personally, it becomes hard to flag-wave with any enthusiasm."

Lord Chamberlain rose and came round from behind his desk.

"Cheer up," he said. "It may not be as bad as you anticipate. I suppose it is too early to offer you a drink?"

"To drown my sorrows, or to celebrate?" the Marquess enquired. "Thank you, but it is too early for either."

He put out his hand.

"Thank you, My Lord, for breaking it as kindly as you could. I now have two months or nine weeks or sixty-one days of freedom left. What is more, I have to spend them looking for the bait which will have me caught, hook, line, and sinker, for the rest of my life!"

The Lord Chamberlain laughed again.

"Whatever else, you have not lost your sense of humour," he said. "If there is anything I can do to help you, let me know."

"You have already done more than enough," the Marquess answered.

The Lord Chamberlain was not certain whether the Marquess was being sarcastic or grateful.

The Marquess picked up his top-hat which he had placed on a chair when he first entered the room.

"Two months!" he said as if to remind himself.

Then he went from the room, closing the door quietly behind him.

The Lord Chamberlain sighed and sat down again at his desk.

He knew that what he had told the Marquess had been a body blow.

He had admired, as everyone else did, his achievements and, above all, his success with horse-flesh.

However envious and jealous any man might be, he never denied that the Marquess rode magnificently.

The horses that were trained under him had all done well.

He could produce the finest horses to be seen either on the race-course or in the hunting-field.

It would be impossible, the Lord Chamberlain knew, to appoint anyone as Master of the Horse who would be in any way the Marquess's equal.

He knew, however, that whatever his opinion on the matter, it would be impossible to change the Queen's mind.

He had daringly remonstrated with her already when she had told him what was the condition for the appointment.

"But the Marquess of Rockingdale, Ma'am, is only twenty-eight," he had argued, "and many men settle down much later than that."

"I am aware of that, Lord Chamberlain," the Queen said sharply, "but the Marquess needs the steadying influence of a wife, and that is something that he certainly lacks at the moment."

The Lord Chamberlain had no idea what had happened, or why Her Majesty had taken up this attitude.

He only knew it would be purposeless to try to discuss the matter further.

He therefore bowed himself out of the room, wishing that somebody else had to break the news to the Marquess.

* * *

As the Marquess drove away from St. James's Palace, he could feel his fury rising within him.

How dare the Queen interfere in his private life!

How dare she insist upon his being married when he had no desire to make any woman his wife!

Of course, as the Lord Chamberlain had said, he could refuse the position.

To do so, however, would inevitably cause a great deal of comment.

Everybody would speculate as to what he had done to upset the Queen.

The whole Family would take it as an insult to them personally.

Too late, as many a man had done before him, he wished he could turn back the clock.

He wished he had not tried to alleviate his boredom by pursuing the pretty Lady Mentmore.

But what was done was done, and now there was really no choice for him to make.

He had to find himself a wife, and he had two months in which to do so.

As he drove up St. James's Street, he was staring straight ahead of him, ignoring the raised hands of several of his friends.

He ignored, too, the inviting smile of a Lady he passed in her open carriage.

He drove down Piccadilly oblivious of everything but his own dark thoughts.

When he reached Rock House in Park Lane he decided that he must have time to think.

He knew when he went into his Study there would be the usual pile of invitations lying on his desk.

As a rule, he accepted only two or three of these.

His Secretary refused the rest.

Now he told himself savagely that if he was to meet the type of Lady of whom the Queen would approve, he must attend the Balls.

There, waiting for him, would be the *débutantes*.

At the parties he usually attended there were no ambitious Mamas speculating as to which partner their daughters danced with would make them suitable husbands.

They would be determining which of them were most eligible having a title.

Alternately, sufficient wealth to keep their daughters in the manner to which they were accustomed.

No, the parties he went to were strictly for married women.

The Marquess could never remember having met a *débutante*.

Occasionally he had seen them sitting meekly beside their Chaperons.

They would be eyeing every man who came near them, hoping he would ask them to dance.

'They will be heavy on their feet and incapable of saying one intelligent word!' the Marquess thought savagely.

He picked up the gold bell which stood on his desk and rang it furiously.

When a footman opened the door, he said sharply:

"Send Mr. Barratt to me!"

When his Secretary, whom he had engaged when he succeeded on his Father's death, came hurrying in, he said:

"I am going to the country, Barratt. Cancel all my invitations for the next two or three days and inform anybody who enquires that I have had to leave London on urgent Family business."

That was the right word for it, he thought angrily.

"Family business" which involved his taking on a wife and eventually a Family he did not want.

After a hasty luncheon, when he found it difficult to swallow anything, despite the fact that his Chef had prepared some of his favourite dishes, he left.

As he climbed into the Travelling Chariot, the servants looked at him apprehensively.

His grooms exchanged glances as he drove his team faster than he habitually did, yet, still with the expertise for which he was famous.

He reached Rock in record time.

For the first time since he had inherited, he felt no thrill of excitement as he went up the drive.

Nor did the beauty of the great building stir his heart as it usually did.

The reason why the Marquess had spent so much time in London after growing up was not entirely because of the attractive women who abounded there.

It was also because he found it more and more impossible to accept the way in which his Father's Estate was managed.

He had served for two years in the Household Cavalry after leaving Oxford.

He had then thought his Father would want him to take over the running of the Estate.

He had hoped he would be allowed to introduce many innovations and new methods.

He considered these to be essential and long overdue.

Unfortunately, however, the Marquess's Father had no intention of allowing what he called "new-fangled ideas" to change in any way his life at Rock.

His son had tried to persuade him that the stables were old and in need of repair.

It would be better, in fact, to demolish them and build new ones with the latest system of ventilation and other improvements.

His Father had been horrified at the idea.

"They were good enough for my Father and his Father before him," he insisted, "and they are good enough for me!"

It was the same objection he had made to every one of his son's suggestions.

Finally he became so frustrated that he went back to London.

He soon found that when not in London he could spend time very pleasantly in Leicestershire.

He owned there a comfortable Hunting-Lodge in which there was plenty of room for his friends.

There was also a house in Newmarket where he could supervise his race-horses.

His Father had made those over to him when he was twenty-one.

Each time he visited Rock it annoyed him more and more that it was so behind the times.

He could not understand why his Father not only tolerated it but clung to it.

For the two years since he had inherited, he had been exclusively occupied in putting into operation all the innovations he had been longing to make.

He had had no time for social contacts with his neighbours.

Nor was he in any way concerned with what was happening in the County.

He was, instead, intent upon installing electric light in the house.

He was building new stables and organising a better system of farming the land which was not let, but managed by the owner of Rock.

He pensioned off the Farmer who had obeyed without question everything the Marquess's Father had told him to do.

This amounted to two words: "No Change."

He replaced him with a young man who believed in fertilisers and the rotation of crops and who was prepared to experiment with live-stock.

The Marquess was interested in bringing in new breeds of sheep.

He bred better cattle than there had ever been on his Father's land.

It all took time.

It meant building new cottages for the old employees he retired and for the new men he took on.

The Marquess enjoyed every minute of it.

Few people outside the Estate had any idea what he was doing.

For he had no intention of acknowledging that his Father had made mistakes.

In that particular part of the country the Marquess was like a Sovereign in his own right.

In fact, Rock was a State within a State.

Over two thousand people were paid on Fridays for their work in the various departments, some old, some new.

The Stonemasons, the Bricklayers, the Painters, the Carpenters had always been there.

But their numbers had gradually dwindled.

Now each one of these departments was seething with young people.

They were eager to contribute new ideas and to work the new methods which their employer demanded.

It was, the Marquess thought, the most exciting thing he had ever done.

What he did not want was to have to share it with some tiresome young woman.

She would not have the least understanding why

he should exert himself in this manner.

He dreaded the very idea of her as he proceeded up the drive.

He was welcomed home by Dawson the Butler, who had been there since he was a boy.

Walking across the Great Hall, the Marquess told himself that this was his, every inch of it.

Why should he want anything more?

To hell with the position of Master of the Horse!

His own horses were far finer than any in the Royal Stables.

He could be content to let Her Majesty look after her own animals without any help from him.

Then he knew that wonderful though Rock was, it was not enough for him.

He wanted more.

He wanted the power that was part of the Monarchy, the power to contribute to the Nation by improving first the horses in the Royal Stables.

Then perhaps he could serve England in some other capacity in which only he could excel.

"I have to do it, I have to!" he told himself.

But he knew with a sinking of his heart that he was not permitted to do it alone.

* * *

The Marquess spent a surprisingly peaceful night.

He had expected to lie awake, worrying over his future.

Instead, because he had already worn himself out, he slept until it was dawn.

He had told his Valet to call him early, but he was up and half-dressed before the man appeared.

"You're early, M'Lord!" the Valet remarked.

"I have a lot to do," the Marquess replied.

The most important thing he had to do, he told himself, was something he did not want to think about.

The Valet knew his Master would want breakfast earlier than expected.

He quickly sent a footman to warn the Chef.

By the time the Marquess entered the Breakfast-Room there were six entree dishes on the side-board.

Dawson was carrying in the silver coffee-pot.

He had known the Marquess long enough to realise that something was wrong.

He was therefore aware that it would be a mistake to be talkative.

He certainly must not ask questions.

He put the coffee-pot down in front of the Marquess, who was sitting at the head of the table and went from the room.

Breakfast was the one meal at which the servants did not wait at table.

That was a tradition, the Marquess thought, not to be changed.

He preferred helping himself, being able to read the newspaper without having people moving about and asking stupid questions.

He was therefore surprised as he started to eat a dish of kidneys and mushrooms when he heard the door open behind him.

" 'Scuse me, M'Lord," Dawson said, "but Lady Athina Ling has called."

"At this hour?" the Marquess exclaimed.

He tried to remember who Lady Athina Ling was.

The name seemed to ring a bell, but for the moment he could not recall her.

"Lady Athina," Dawson said respectfully, "is th' daughter of th' late Earl of Murling whose Estate marches with Your Lordship's."

"Oh, yes, of course," the Marquess answered.

"Her Ladyship apologises for disturbing you so early, M'Lord, but she says it's on a very urgent matter."

The Marquess decided it would be rude to send her away.

He therefore replied:

"Tell Lady Athina I will see her as soon as I have finished my breakfast, but I am, in fact, going riding."

"I'll inform Her Ladyship," Dawson replied.

He went from the room.

The Marquess deliberately poured himself another cup of coffee.

"What can the damned woman want at this hour of the morning?" he asked.

He wanted to ride over his own land, on his own horse, and try to clear his thoughts.

He did not want to talk to anybody—he wanted just to think.

He had, nevertheless, the uncomfortable feeling that however much he thought about the dilemma he was in, there was no solution.

chapter four

ONLY as she walked up the steps to the front-door did Athina realise that it was much too early for anybody to make a call.

She had been so afraid that Lord Burnham might overtake her and snatch Peter away.

She had thought of nothing but reaching Rock as a place of safety.

The door was opened by a footman.

When she entered, a grey-haired Butler came forward.

"I should be grateful if I could see the Marquess of Rockingdale immediately," she said. "It is on a very urgent matter."

Thinking the Butler looked slightly sceptical, she continued:

"I am Lady Athina Ling."

The man's face lit up, and he said:

"Of course, M'Lady. I remember th' late Earl coming here often."

He went ahead and showed her into a Study.

There were some fine pictures of horses by Stubbs on the walls.

The room contained comfortable masculine furniture covered in red leather.

The Butler went out of the room and Peter said:

"Is it my Uncle we are going to see? I do not think I remember him."

"I expect you will when you see him again," Athina said confidently.

She nearly added: "He must have been at your Mother's Funeral," then thought that might upset Peter.

Instead, she went on:

"This is a beautiful house, and I am sure your Mother loved playing in these big rooms when she was a little girl."

"She used to tell me about the swing in the garden, and a little house in the trees," Peter said as if he were just recalling it.

The Butler came back to say:

"His Lordship'll see you, M'Lady, as soon as 'e's finished 'is breakfast."

"Thank you," Athina replied, "and as I would like to speak to him alone, I wonder if it would be possible to give Lady Louise's son, who is here with me, something to eat? We have come a long way and I am sure he is both hungry and thirsty."

"Master Peter!" the Butler exclaimed. "I wondered who the young gentleman was and thought 'e resembled someone I knew. Of course, 'tis Lady Louise!"

He was obviously excited at meeting Peter and, putting out his hand, he said:

"If you'll come with me, Master Peter, I'll give you some breakfast and show you th' secret safe in my Pantry which your Mother used to love when she was your age."

Peter looked interested.

"Why is it a secret?" he asked.

They went from the room.

Athina could hear the Butler telling Peter about the silver-safe as they went down the passage.

She walked to the window to look out at the lake a little way below the house.

She could see swans and ducks swimming in it.

Beyond it in the Park through which they had just driven were the spotted deer.

It was all so beautiful and looked so peaceful.

It seemed incredible that one of the Family, so young and so vulnerable, should be treated in such a horrifying manner.

The door opened and the Marquess came in.

Athina turned round slowly.

She thought at a quick glance that he was younger and more handsome than she had expected.

She had no idea that the Marquess was astonished at her looks.

She was so very different from what he had expected.

He walked across the room and held out his hand.

"How do you do, Lady Athina," he said. "I do not think we have ever met, but I remember your Father well. I was extremely sorry to learn of his death."

"As you can imagine, I miss him very much," Athina replied.

"What can I do for you?" the Marquess asked in a brisk tone. "I expect Dawson, my Butler, has told you that I was just about to go riding."

"I would not have called so early," Athina explained, "if it had not been of the utmost importance and concerns your nephew, Peter Naver."

The Marquess looked surprised.

"What has he been up to?" he asked. "And how does it concern you?"

Athina sat down on a sofa which stood near the fireplace.

"Last night," she began, "I had to stay at a Posting-Inn called the Crown and Feathers. While I was having dinner I noticed a Gentleman who was being noisily aggressive with a small boy."

"You were staying alone?" the Marquess asked unexpectedly.

"I had had a slight accident to the wheel of my Chaise," Athina replied, "and was unable to proceed until early this morning."

She thought the interruption was unnecessary and went on:

"I was just going to sleep when I heard a small boy, who I afterwards learnt was your nephew, screaming in the next room."

The Marquess frowned.

"Why was he screaming?"

"He was screaming," Athina replied, "because his Stepfather, who I understand is Lord Burnham, was furious because he had gone to the stables to

76

comfort a horse that Lord Burnham had whipped on the journey."

She paused a moment and this time the Marquess did not say anything.

"To punish him," Athina continued, "he whipped the boy unmercifully until he was almost unconscious."

There was silence while the Marquess stared at Athina as if he could hardly credit what she was saying.

Then he said:

"I cannot believe that my brother-in-law could be so cruel as you imply. After all, small boys often require correction. There is nothing unusual about their being spanked."

"This was no question of being 'spanked,'" Athina said sharply. "He was beaten unmercifully with a whip which left open weals on his skin."

The Marquess walked across the room to his desk, then back again before he said:

"I quite understand, Lady Athina, that you were upset, but I assure you, most boys get whipped at some time or another. I have always believed that my nephew is being well looked after by his Stepfather. It would be incorrect for me to interfere in his upbringing."

Athina rose to her feet.

She was thinking her Father had been right in everything he had said about the Marquess.

She had slept very little last night and was tired from the journey.

Now she felt her temper rising.

She did not speak, however, but walked towards the door.

"Where are you going?" the Marquess asked as she reached it.

Athina turned back.

"As you have lived up to your reputation, My Lord," she said, "I will tell you exactly what I am doing. I am taking Peter to Windsor Castle. I will show the Queen how brutally a Peer of the Realm has marked the child and will warn her that her new Master of the Horse is likely to treat Her Majesty's own horses in the same manner."

If she had thrown a bomb at the Marquess, he could not have been more surprised.

Never in his whole life had a woman spoken to him in such a manner.

It seemed incredible that anyone so small, so fragile and beautiful, should so insult him.

Athina started to open the door.

He realised abruptly that she would undoubtedly do what she had said.

She would go to Windsor Castle, and he was well aware of the damage it would cause him.

Quickly he walked towards her, saying:

"Forgive me, Lady Athina, if I sounded callous. Of course I am concerned about my sister's child."

Athina stood still, but she did not speak, and he said again:

"Please forgive me, and let us discuss this sensibly. I am convinced now you are not exaggerating the situation, as I first thought."

Slowly and somewhat reluctantly Athina closed the door again.

She turned back into the room.

As she did, she looked at the Marquess and he knew he had never seen a woman look at him with such contempt.

He found it hard to believe that she disliked him as much as she appeared to do.

"Come and sit down," he said in his most engaging tone.

Again slowly, as if she were only half persuaded to do so, Athina walked back to the place she had vacated on the sofa.

"Now let us start from the beginning," the Marquess suggested, "and try to forget I said all the wrong things and upset you."

He had never met a woman who did not succumb when he pleaded with her.

He was aware, however, that Athina was sitting very straight and stiff on the edge of the sofa.

He could feel her hostility vibrating from her.

"Let me explain," the Marquess continued, "that when my sister died, she left her son in the charge of her second husband, Lord Burnham."

Athina made no comment and he went on:

"In fact, she made a Will, leaving her money, which amounted to a considerable sum, since she had a private fortune left her by her Godfather, to Peter with Lord Burnham as the administrator of it until Peter reached the age of twenty-one."

He paused, then added as if trying to remember the exact wording that had been used:

"If anything happened to Peter before then, the money was to go to Lord Burnham and not back to the Family, as we might have expected."

Now he made a little gesture with his hand before he said:

"You can understand why I was not concerned in any way as to where my nephew lived or what he did. Nor have any of my relatives, who have seen him, made any complaints as to the manner in which he is being treated."

Even as he spoke, the Marquess remembered something.

Someone had told him that Burnham had been short of cash before his wife died.

Perhaps it was a chance remark, because he could not recall who had said it.

Nor had it made any real impact on him at the time.

Now, however, it struck him that it was, of course, extremely convenient for his brother-in-law to have the care of a child who was so rich.

There was still no response from Athina.

After a moment the Marquess said:

"I will, of course, speak to Lord Burnham and tell him of your complaint, and we can only hope that he will be kinder to the boy in the future."

"I heard the way in which Lord Burnham was behaving last night," Athina said slowly, "and I would not allow any child, not even one who is older and stronger than Peter, to be in that brute's care for another five minutes!"

She drew in her breath before she said:

"I brought Peter here to you because I thought you would save him and protect him. If you refuse to do anything, then I will! Even if it means taking Peter to Windsor, or going abroad with him."

The Marquess looked bewildered.

"I do not quite understand," he said. "Are you saying you have brought the boy here to me?"

"I thought your Butler would have told you," Athina said. "I smuggled him away at five o'clock this morning. We have driven at great speed because I was afraid Lord Burnham would overtake me."

She saw the Marquess was still looking puzzled, and she explained:

"We had no time for breakfast and, as I wanted to speak to you alone, your Butler has taken Peter to have something to eat."

"In that case," the Marquess said, "before we go any further, I would like to meet my nephew."

Athina rose from the sofa with her head held high.

The Marquess hurried to open the door for her.

She was disliking him for not being appalled by cruelty to children.

They walked down the corridor towards the hall.

The Marquess was wondering where Dawson had taken the boy, when the Butler appeared.

"If you're looking for Master Peter, M'Lady," he said to Athina, "I gave 'im some breakfast, but 'e couldn't eat much because 'is back was hurting 'im.

So I've taken 'im upstairs to Mrs. Field. She'll know what to do."

"Mrs. Field is my Housekeeper," the Marquess explained quickly.

"Thank you," Athina said to the Butler. "I would like to go up to him."

"I will take you," the Marquess said.

They walked up the impressive staircase side by side.

When they reached the First Floor, the Marquess turned left.

They walked a long way down a wide corridor.

He opened a door covered in green baize which Athina knew would lead into the Servants' part of the house.

After they had passed through it, he opened another door on the right-hand side of the corridor.

They walked into a Sitting-Room where the sunshine was pouring in through the windows.

Peter was standing in front of one of them in his trousers and without his shirt.

An elderly woman with a kind face was examining his back.

When he saw Athina come into the room, Peter gave a cry and ran to her.

He held out his arms and Athina went down on her knees.

As he flung himself against her, she pulled off her hat so that it was easier to kiss him.

He put his arms round her neck and his cheek against hers.

"I thought . . . you had . . . gone . . . away," he said.

"No, no, of course I would not do that," Athina comforted him. "I am here and I understand your back is hurting you."

"It itched . . . and . . . itched," Peter said. "I wanted to . . . scratch it . . . but I . . . could not . . . reach."

As he spoke, Athina heard Mrs. Field say to the Marquess:

"Never in all me born years, M'Lord, have I seen anything so wicked and horrible as th' way this little boy's been treated. It's enough to make Her Ladyship turn in her grave!"

The Marquess had moved round so that he could see Peter's back where the light from the window shone on it.

If anything, it looked worse than it had last night.

During the drive several of the weals had bled and had stuck to his shirt.

The skin surrounding them was red and swollen.

He could also see what Athina had seen, that there were old scars from previous beatings.

"You will . . . not leave me . . . will . . . you?" Peter was asking.

He was almost in tears and speaking in a whisper, but the Marquess heard.

"I promise I will not do that," Athina assured him, "but you must let this kind lady put some cream on your back which I should have done this morning. It was stupid of me not to, but I was in such a hurry to get away."

"We escaped . . . from Step-Papa," Peter murmured.

"Yes, we escaped," Athina agreed.

"And you do not . . . think . . . Step-Papa will find . . . me . . . here?"

There was a note of terror in Peter's voice.

Athina looked up at the Marquess, who was standing behind him.

"I can answer that question," the Marquess said, "and I promise you that your Stepfather will never beat you again."

There was a hard note in his voice.

If there was one thing the Marquess loathed, it was cruelty.

He had once knocked a man down on the race-course for beating a horse that had not won a race he had been expected to win.

He had been challenged by a member of White's Club to a duel because he had accused him of ill-treating one of his carriage-horses.

The Marquess saw Athina's eyes light up as if the sunshine were in them.

It suddenly struck him that kneeling on the floor with Peter's arms around her, she looked very lovely.

With her head close to Peter's, she might have stepped from a picture painted by a great Master of the Madonna and Child.

After he had spoken, Peter loosened his tight hold on Athina.

He turned his face round to look at the Marquess.

"This is your Uncle," Athina said. "He knows that we ran away and I have brought you here for his protection."

She looked at the Marquess quizzically as she spoke.

The Marquess held out his hand.

"I am delighted to meet you, Peter," he said, "and I think it was very clever of you to run away with Lady Athina. Now I have to talk to her about what we are going to do in the future."

"I will . . . not have . . . to go . . . back to . . . Step-Papa . . . will I?" Peter asked in a quavering voice.

"I promise you will not have to do that," the Marquess replied.

He looked at Mrs. Field.

"Now, suppose you work your magic on Master Peter's back," he said, "while I take Her Ladyship downstairs to have some breakfast."

"I'll do that, M'Lord," Mrs. Field said. "I've already promised the young gent'man he'll feel quite different when I've put some honey on his wound."

"Honey?" Athina exclaimed. "Will that take away the pain?"

"He'll have no pain an' these terrible scars will heal in two days!" Mrs. Field assured her.

"I have never heard of anybody using honey before," Athina said.

"My Ma were known as a White Witch," Mrs. Field answered, "and people came from far and wide to get th' herbal remedies she made for 'em. But she allus said that when it come to healin' cuts, there's nothin' like honey, an' I allus uses it meself."

"What do you think of that, Peter?" the Marquess exclaimed. "You have a White Witch looking after you, and who could ask for more?"

Peter looked at Mrs. Field wide-eyed.

"Do you fly on a broomstick?" he asked.

"I wishes I could!" she replied. "That's wot they used to say me Ma did, and that's wot you'll want t'do when your back's healed! So come on, and let me put some honey on it."

Athina rose to her feet.

"Stay with Mrs. Field until she has finished," she said, "and I will be downstairs, waiting for you."

Peter put out his hand to touch her.

"You . . . promise? You will not go . . . away without . . . me?"

"I promise," Athina said after another glance at the Marquess.

She picked up her hat which she had put down on the floor.

Then she said to Mrs. Field:

"Thank you, thank you very much. I am very grateful!"

She saw that Mrs. Field was about to put what looked like thick clover honey on strips of linen.

They would cover Peter's injuries held in place by a bandage.

The Marquess opened the door and they walked out into the corridor.

She thought he would say something, but they went on in silence down the stairs and into the Breakfast-Room.

Dawson must have anticipated that was what they would do.

He was just placing a silver coffee-pot on a tray at the top of the table.

"You say you left at five o'clock," the Marquess said. "You must be starving by now."

"I admit to feeling a trifle hungry," Athina said, "but usually one becomes thirsty when driving because of the dust."

She remembered, as she spoke, how Peter had said that his Stepfather would not let him stop for a drink of water yesterday.

She felt there was no point in giving further instances of the cruelty the child had suffered.

It was enough that the Marquess had seen his back.

He walked to the sideboard and lifted the lids of some of the entree dishes.

"Will you have eggs or fish, or both?" he asked.

Athina gave a little laugh.

"I think a little of both would be very nice."

She sat down at the table and he brought them to her.

Then he poured out some coffee for her and another for himself, saying as he did so:

"There is no need for me to admit in words that I was wrong and you were absolutely right."

"I thought you would agree with me when you saw for yourself what has been happening to Peter," Athina said. "I suppose it would have been more sensible to let you see him first."

She thought, as she spoke, that they were each

conceding something to the other.

Her common sense told her that if she was to fight for Peter, it was essential to have the Marquess on her side.

He was obviously thinking, and she remained silent until he said:

"Do you think Burnham will follow you?"

"I was thinking on the way here that he would," Athina answered, "once he realised there was a communicating-door between Peter's room and mine. He had locked Peter's outside door, so he would know Peter must have left with me."

She paused for a moment before she added:

"He will learn that I left very early, but he will not know who I am."

"Why is that?" the Marquess asked.

"Because I gave the Proprietor the name of my Chaperon, Mrs. Beckwith," Athina explained.

She hesitated for a moment before she said:

"But my groom was wearing my Father's livery, and there were other grooms there who might have recognised it."

The Marquess nodded.

"I should think that is more than likely. Burnham, who has, of course, often stayed here, might easily be aware that our Estates march with each other."

Athina stiffened.

"In which case he will go straight to Murling Park. What shall I . . . do? What shall I . . . say if he . . . comes?"

She felt suddenly rather helpless.

The servants were old, and she remembered how aggressive and loud-voiced Lord Burnham had been.

She felt that she and Mrs. Beckwith would not be able to cope with him.

She was suddenly frightened, so frightened that she forgot for a moment her dislike of the Marquess and said pleadingly:

"I promised Peter he should not go . . . back with him and also that I would not . . . leave him. Tell me what I should do . . . please . . . tell me!"

"Peter will stay here," the Marquess said firmly, "and I will cope with Burnham. At the same time, as I am unmarried, there is every possibility that he will assert I am not a suitable person to be in charge of a child."

As he spoke the word "unmarried," the Marquess had an idea.

For the moment it seemed so inconceivable that he could hardly formulate it to himself.

Then, as he tried to do so, the door opened and Peter came in.

He was not wearing a coat, but he had on a clean white shirt.

Athina guessed Mrs. Field had found one which had once belonged to the Marquess when he was a small boy.

Peter walked towards her, saying:

"My back . . . feels better . . . much . . . much better . . . already!"

He stood beside Athina's chair and looked at what was on her plate.

"The Butler said you ate very little at breakfast," Athina said, "and now that you are feeling better, perhaps you would like some more?"

"Can I have some more?" Peter asked. "Step-Papa never allowed me to have a second helping, and when he says I have been naughty, I have no food for a whole day."

"That must make you feel very hungry," Athina remarked.

"I have a big hole in my tummy," Peter replied, "and sometimes I feel so weak that it is difficult to get out of bed."

Athina looked at the Marquess.

Although it seemed strange, she knew she could read his thoughts.

They were both thinking the same thing.

It was so incredible that she almost dismissed it as pure imagination.

She knew, however, beyond all doubt, that the same idea had occurred to Peter's Uncle.

"Well, Peter, now that you are here with me," the Marquess said aloud, "you are to eat big meals every day, otherwise you will not be strong enough to ride my horses."

"Ride your horses?" Peter repeated. "Can I do that?"

"Of course you can," the Marquess promised. "Your Father was a very good rider and I expect you are too."

He rose from the table as he spoke and lifted the lids of the entree dishes in the same way that he had for Athina.

This time, however, he lifted more of them.

"Now you have to eat all this," he said to Peter, "and if this is not enough, we will tell the Chef to make you some more."

Peter laughed.

"If I eat all that, I will get so fat that I will be too heavy for your horses to carry me!"

"We will risk it," the Marquess replied, "and if my horses cannot manage you, we will try the ones that draw the carts."

Peter laughed as if it were a huge joke.

Athina thought that the Marquess at least was clever in gaining the confidence of the small boy.

He piled Peter's plate with food and poured him out some milk.

Then he sat down again at the head of the table.

As he did so, Athina said:

"As I have finished, My Lord, I would like to have another word with you about where we should go and what we should do."

"Yes, of course," the Marquess agreed.

Peter looked up from the other end of the table as Athina rose.

"You are . . . not leaving . . . me?" he asked in a nervous voice.

"I am just going back to the Study with your Uncle," Athina said. "I am sure Dawson will come in and tell you more about what your Mother enjoyed when she was a little girl."

The Marquess had already rung the bell while Athina was still speaking.

"Master Peter is very hungry, Dawson," the Marquess said. "I have told him he is to eat up everything he can so that he will be strong enough to ride the biggest of my horses."

"I'm sure he'll soon do that, M'Lord," Dawson said.

"Now, see he has everything he wants," the Marquess went on, "and when he has finished, you can bring him to the Study."

"Very good, M'Lord, and I'll look after Master Peter," Dawson replied.

Athina stopped just long enough to smooth Peter's hair back and drop a kiss on his forehead.

"There is no hurry," she said softly. "You are going to stay here, and anyway, I do not think your Stepfather will find us for a long time."

She felt, as she spoke, Peter's relief as he let out a deep sigh.

It seemed to seep through his small body.

She knew the child was terrified of being beaten again.

As she and the Marquess reached the Study, he shut the door before he said:

"I have a proposition to put to you. I only hope it will not make you angry again."

"I am not angry now that I know you realise how much Peter has suffered and that it cannot go on," Athina replied quietly.

She was silent for a moment.

Then she said in a very low voice:

"I . . . I knew what you were . . . thinking just now . . . and I was thinking the same thing . . . that his Stepfather is trying to . . . kill him!"

"It did pass through my mind," the Marquess admitted. "But how could any man in his position even think of such a dreadful thing as murdering a little boy?"

"You can see how thin Peter is," Athina insisted, "and the terrible injuries that have been inflicted on his back. Not only is he terrified, but he has also been deprived of food and drink—"

"I realise that," the Marquess interrupted, "and it makes me so angry that it would give me the greatest pleasure to give my brother-in-law a taste of his own medicine."

He spoke savagely, then in a different tone he said:

"At the same time, he is a much older man than I am, and it would be a mistake, whatever else we do, to create any kind of a scandal."

"Are you afraid it would damage your reputation?" Athina asked somewhat sarcastically.

"I was not actually thinking of myself," the Marquess answered, "but of my Family. As you can imagine, if it becomes known what has been happening, there will be an uproar, and as his Guardian, Burnham will make things more unpleasant for us than we could for him."

"I understand what you are saying," Athina replied, "but I am thinking only of Peter."

"I have a solution to the problem, and that is what I want to explain to you," the Marquess said.

"I am listening," Athina answered.

She sat down in the same place on the sofa where she had sat before, with both hands in her lap.

The Marquess stood with his back to the fire-place. Then he said:

"If you think you have a problem, Lady Athina, so have I. What I am going to tell you is strictly confidential, and I feel sure you will not repeat it to anybody else."

Athina nodded and he went on:

"I was informed yesterday by the Lord Chamberlain that Her Majesty the Queen will appoint me Master of the Horse only on the condition that I am married or engaged to be."

Athina stared at him.

"But, as I told you, I have always understood that it was a tradition that the Head of your Family should hold that position. At least that is what my Father told me."

"That is true," the Marquess agreed, "but the decision as to who occupies the post is, of course, for Her Majesty to make."

Athina wondered how this concerned Peter, and she asked:

"What are you going to do about it?"

"I was thinking it might be dangerous for you to take Peter to your home, as I think you intended," the Marquess said. "He can stay here, but I think my brother-in-law will protest."

He paused a moment and then continued:

"As I am much younger than he is, and, of course, unmarried, he could claim that he is a far more suitable Guardian for the boy than I am."

As if Athina had become suddenly aware of where this conversation was leading, she stiffened.

"What I am suggesting," the Marquess went on, "is that for Peter's sake and mine, you agree to an engagement between us which—"

"No! No! Of course not!" Athina interrupted. "I vowed a long time ago that I would never marry anybody unless I was in love with them! I can only say, My Lord—and I do not wish to be rude—that I would not marry you under any circumstances!"

"I have no wish to be married myself," the Marquess said, "and if you had allowed me, Lady Athina, to finish my sentence, I was going to say an engagement which we privately agree can be terminated at any time that suits either of us."

Athina stared at him. Then she said:

"Do you mean . . . it will just be a . . . pretence?"

"Of course that is what I mean," the Marquess said, "for if you have no wish to be married, no more do I."

He looked at her a moment and then went on:

"However, to announce our engagement could make me Master of the Horse and at the same time enable you to stay here, with, of course, your Chaperon, until such time as Lord Burnham accepts that he is no longer Peter's Guardian."

Athina pressed her hands together.

Now she understood exactly what the Marquess was proposing.

She could see that from Peter's point of view it was the only way he could be safe and she could be with him.

As it also solved the Marquess's problem, there

was no reason for her to be afraid that she would become too involved with him.

Nor was there any reason—and this was vitally important—that she might eventually be forced into marrying him.

He was watching the changing expression on her face, and quite unexpectedly she exclaimed:

"That is a very clever idea! I see now exactly what you mean, and of course Lord Burnham could have no valid objection to your future wife wanting to have charge of Peter. Your family also will accept it as the natural thing to do."

"That is what I thought myself," the Marquess said in a tone of satisfaction. "Then when the danger is past and Burnham is no longer a threat, you can say that you find me intolerable and break off the engagement—a thing which I would be unable to do."

"Do you really mean that I can stay here for the time being?" Athina asked eagerly.

"I should be delighted to have you as my guest, with the Chaperon you said you had living with you at Murling Park."

"Mrs. Beckwith is a charming and delightful person, and a great authority on the Geography of the world. I think you will find her very interesting. She is, incidentally, the daughter of the Bishop of Oxford."

The Marquess laughed.

"That is certainly a good cover. It might be part of a plot in a Drury Lane Drama!"

"I would almost enjoy it if it were not for Peter,"

Athina said. "You do see the terrible way in which he has been . . . treated?"

Her voice broke on the last word, and the Marquess said:

"Only a Devil could treat a small child like that! I only wish to God I had known about it earlier. I promise you, Lady Athina, I would kill that man sooner than let him touch Louise's son again!"

He spoke with a sincerity that Athina knew was genuine.

"I am sure Peter will be happy here," she said, "and if we both love him as he wants to be loved, he will forget what has happened to him this past year."

"What I cannot understand," the Marquess said, "is why my relatives, who are usually so nosey and miss nothing of what goes on, had no idea what Burnham was like, or how that child has been tortured by him."

"I think it would be a mistake to under-estimate Lord Burnham," Athina said. "I thought him a loud and unpleasant bully even before I heard him beating Peter, and if it is a question of money, which is always at the root of all evil, I think he will fight to get Peter back."

She sighed before she went on:

"He might take even more drastic steps!"

"Now you are frightening me," the Marquess protested, "and I refuse to be frightened! The man is a monster and sooner or later will get his just deserts. But meanwhile you and I have to be clever about this."

"We must certainly try," Athina said.

The Marquess sat down on the sofa beside her.

"So you agree," he said, "that we announce to the world, or rather to my Family and the Lord Chamberlain, that we are engaged to be married."

He smiled at her before he continued:

"It will be published in the *London Gazette*. We will immediately send over to Murling Park for your Chaperon and, of course, for what clothes you will require while you are staying here."

He paused for breath, then added:

"I will get my Secretary to start writing at once to my relations to tell them the 'good news.' "

Athina was listening. Then she said:

"I can see you are an organiser and I am therefore content to leave these things in your hands. All I am concerned with at the moment is to make Peter happy and to protect him."

She met the Marquess's eyes as she spoke.

She knew he was thinking, as she was, that Lord Burnham would not give in easily.

chapter five

"Do you know, Uncle Denzil," Peter said as they sat round the table at luncheon, "that Michelangelo was the first person to know what a horse looked like inside. He made a drawing of it."

"I suppose Mrs. Beckwith showed you that in one of the books in the Library," the Marquess replied.

He looked across the table at Mrs. Beckwith and asked:

"Does that come under History or Geography?"

Mrs. Beckwith's eyes twinkled.

"It comes, My Lord, under 'useful Hints for Horse-Breeders.' "

"Breeders?" the Marquess queried.

"I am going to breed the finest horse in the world," Peter cried. "His father will be *Samson* while his mother will be Aunt Athina's *Juno*. He will win the Grand National and I will ride him."

The Marquess laughed.

"That is certainly an ambitious programme!"

He turned to Athina, who was sitting next to him, and said:

"You did not tell me you owned a good breeding-mare."

"I have, in fact, quite a number," she answered.

The Marquess raised his eye-brows.

"Why did you not tell me about them?"

"I thought," she replied, "that it would be presuming on Xanadu."

The Marquess laughed again.

"Is that how you think of Rock?"

"Of course," she replied, "and you are undoubtedly Kublai Khan."

"He should wear a crown," Peter said. "When Mrs. Beckwith read me the poem, I was quite sure that Kublai Khan would wear a crown."

The Marquess thought it was all quite extraordinary.

During the last four days the conversation at meals had been full of wit and wisdom.

It was something he had never imagined could take place between two women and a small boy.

Athina had been right when she had said that Mrs. Beckwith was extremely intelligent, and so indeed was she.

Peter was already a different child from what he had been on his arrival.

He was eating well and spent every minute he could in the stables with the horses.

The Marquess had, to his delight, already mounted him on one of them.

He decided that Athina and Peter would ride

with him every morning, either before or after breakfast.

There had been no sign of Lord Burnham.

Gradually they ceased to be tense and on edge.

Now they were all laughing.

The Marquess was teasing Peter about his intention to win the Grand National, when Dawson came in.

He walked up to the Marquess's side and said:

"Lord Burnham is here, M'Lord, and I've shown him into th' Study."

There was a moment's complete silence.

Then Peter gave a scream of terror.

He jumped from his chair and ran to the Marquess, holding on to him frantically.

"You will . . . not let . . . him take . . . me away? Oh, please . . . Uncle Denzil . . . promise you . . . will not . . . make . . . me go . . . with him."

The Marquess put his arm round the boy.

"I have already promised you that," he replied in a quiet voice. "Now I want you to be brave and not make a scene, but go upstairs with Mrs. Beckwith and stay in your Sitting-Room until I send for you."

"You will . . . not listen . . . to him when he . . . tells you . . . that I want . . . to be with . . . him like . . . he told . . . Grandmama?"

"No, of course not," the Marquess answered. "You must trust me, Peter. I want you to live here with Aunt Athina and me."

Athina rose as he spoke and came round the table.

Peter turned towards her and hid his face in her breast.

"I am . . . frightened!" he whispered. "Very, very . . . frightened!"

"You have to trust your Uncle," she said.

As she spoke, she went down on her knees and held him close against her.

It was the same attitude she had had the first morning when she and the Marquess had gone up to the Housekeeper's room.

He had thought then that she looked like a Madonna.

Now, as he saw the love in her eyes, he thought that was how every woman should look at a child.

"You are all right, you are quite safe," Athina was saying. "Now, go upstairs with Mrs. Beckwith, and use the side staircase so that nobody will see you."

Dawson had said that Lord Burnham was waiting in the Study.

Nevertheless, Athina thought it would be a mistake to take any chances.

Mrs. Beckwith put out her hand and Peter went with her.

Both Athina and the Marquess knew that he was terrified and near to tears.

"Do you really want me to come with you?" Athina asked when they were alone.

"You know it is essential."

"I think I am almost as frightened as Peter," Athina said in a low voice.

"Leave everything to me," the Marquess answered.

He rose from the table and they walked towards the door.

Athina thought it was impossible for there to be so much at stake just because of one man's cruelty.

She felt it would destroy Peter if his Stepfather got control of him.

It would also break her heart and Mrs. Beckwith's.

She had told Athina only this morning that she had never known a more attractive and charming little boy.

"Peter is a joy to teach," she said.

Besides this, Athina had the feeling that the Marquess himself was growing more and more fond of his nephew every day.

There was certainly no sign of his wishing to return to London.

He spent a great deal of his time with Peter.

In the evenings the conversation between him, Mrs. Beckwith, and herself was sparkling and usually very amusing.

She had to admit it was a joy to be able to talk to the Marquess in the same way that she had talked to her Father.

He, however, was full of ideas that would never have entered the Earl's head.

It was the Marquess who had suggested that Peter should call her "Aunt Athina."

It made her concern for him more obvious.

At the same time, they had both been aware that eventually Lord Burnham would catch up with them.

Now it had happened.

Athina felt that the ceiling had fallen in on her head and the walls were crumbling around her.

Without speaking, she and the Marquess walked towards the Study and a footman opened the door.

The Marquess went in first.

Lord Burnham, looking large, aggressive, and red-faced, was standing with his back to the fireplace.

He appeared somewhat debauched as if, Athina thought, he had been drinking.

"Good-afternoon, Roland!" the Marquess said. "I rather expected you would turn up sooner or later."

They did not shake hands. Lord Burnham was looking at Athina.

The Marquess turned to her.

"Let me, my Dear, introduce my brother-in-law, Lord Burnham," he said, "and we must ask him to congratulate us."

"Congratulate you?" Lord Burnham asked.

"Lady Athina Ling and I are engaged," the Marquess explained. "The announcement will appear in the *Gazette* tomorrow morning."

"I have, in fact, been to Murling Park," Lord Burnham said, "in search of a woman called Beckwith who I understand kidnapped my Stepson when I was staying at a Posting-Inn."

He glowered at Athina and continued:

"But from the description I had of Mrs. Beckwith, I think now it was Lady Athina for whom I should have been looking."

"I am sorry if you were perturbed at Peter's dis-appearance," Athina said, "but he was very unhap-py and I thought it essential that the terrible dam-age you had inflicted to his back should have prop-er attention."

"How dare you take him away like that!" Lord Burnham bellowed.

The Marquess held up his hand.

"Do not get into one of your rages," he admon-ished. "My fiancée did exactly the right thing in bringing Peter to me. I was appalled by the ter-rible weals on the child's back. I simply cannot understand how you could have treated him so brutally!"

"Boys need to be disciplined," Lord Burnham blustered. "If he was in as bad a way as Lady Athina thought, she should have told me what she was doing. I have had a Devil of a job trying to find out what had happened to my Stepson."

"How did you discover his whereabouts?" the Marquess asked in a genial tone.

As he spoke, he indicated with his hand that Athina should sit down.

She sat on the edge of the sofa, where he had first talked to her.

The Marquess sat on the arm of one of the chairs.

He supported himself by putting his arm across the back of it.

Athina knew because he seemed so at ease that Lord Burnham was slightly nonplussed.

"What I discovered," he announced, "after a great deal of trouble to myself, was that my Valet thought he recognised the livery of the groom on the Chaise in which Peter must have been taken away. Unfortunately it took him some time to put a name to it."

He took a deep breath before he went on:

"When finally I knew that it belonged to the late Earl of Murling, I drove to Murling Park, intending to interrogate Mrs. Beckwith."

"That was when you learned that she had come here with Lady Athina, as her Chaperon," the Marquess said in a tone of satisfaction.

"I have come here," Lord Burnham corrected himself, "to take my Stepson back to where he belongs, which is in *my* house."

"I am afraid that is impossible," the Marquess said. "He is very happy and content here, and my fiancée loves having him with us."

He smiled at Athina before he went on:

"He is being taught by Mrs. Beckwith, who is one of the most intelligent women I have ever met, and his back is gradually healing and returning to normal."

He said the last sentence very slowly and Lord Burnham did not meet his eyes.

"Perhaps I was a little too harsh," he said after a moment, "but the boy was continually disobedient, spending time with the horses instead of doing other things that were required of him."

"His love of horses comes, of course, from his Father," the Marquess replied, "and from my sister who, as you know, rode extremely well. I can imagine nothing that would please her more than that her son should be here with me, riding my horses."

"I dispute that," Lord Burnham said aggressively. "Your sister in her Will left Peter in my charge and I insist on carrying out her wishes. I intend to have no nonsense from you or anybody else!"

Now there was a look in his eyes which told Athina that his temper was definitely rising.

"Did you really think I would return my nephew, who is not very strong, to you to be beaten until he is almost insensible?" the Marquess asked. "If so, you are very much mistaken! He is staying here with my fiancée and me, and once we are married, we will bring him up with our own children."

"You will do nothing of the sort!" Lord Burnham roared. "Louise gave Peter into my care, and as his Stepfather, I am his natural Guardian. If I go to law over this, you know as well as I do that they will agree that I must carry out the wishes expressed in your sister's Will."

"I think not," the Marquess said slowly, almost drawling the words. "I have asked my Solicitors to discover when the Will was made, and I am informed that it was signed by my sister and witnessed just four days before she died."

He paused, and as Lord Burnham did not speak, he went on:

"A number of my relatives visited her during that last week, who will confirm that she was only semi-conscious and incapable of conversing with them."

"That is untrue!" Lord Burnham shouted.

"They would be prepared to say that on oath," the Marquess continued, "and the Doctors and Nurses who attended my sister would also be called upon to give evidence."

Listening and watching Lord Burnham, Athina realised how very astute the Marquess was being.

The older man seemed to shrink, and there was no bluster left in him.

Instead, he said in a surly manner:

"That child has cost me a great deal of money!"

"Which, of course, will be reimbursed to you," the Marquess said, "but I intend to ask that my sister's fortune be held in trust for the boy. We will work out an arrangement without your having the administration of it solely in your hands, as you have had up until now."

Lord Burnham clenched his fists.

For a moment Athina thought he was going to strike the Marquess.

Then he exclaimed furiously:

"Curse you! May you rot in Hell, and the boy with you!"

As he spoke, furiously and ferociously, Lord Burnham walked past the Marquess and reached the door.

He pulled it open, then turned back.

"I will get even with you, Denzil, sooner or later!" he snarled.

He went out into the corridor, slamming the door behind him.

Athina put her hands up to her face.

The tension had been intolerable, and even now she could hardly believe they had won.

The Marquess raised himself from the arm of the chair.

"It might have been worse," he said coolly.

Then he looked at Athina.

"You are all right?" he asked.

"I feel as if I have been battered by a tornado," she said, "but you were wonderful! I am sure he realises that he can never have Peter back."

"I hope so," the Marquess said quietly.

"How could you guess so cleverly that he had written the Will himself when your sister was dying? I suppose he guided her hand so that she could sign it."

"I have always thought it strange," the Marquess said, "that Louise should have left her son, whom she adored, to be looked after by his Stepfather rather than any of our female relatives who I know would have been only too willing to have him."

"Yet . . . you did . . . nothing about it!"

"There appeared to be no reason why I should," the Marquess said a little guiltily. "I knew Burnham was a somewhat aggressive chap, but it is only lately that he has taken to drinking so heavily, and I have the uncomfortable suspicion that it was because he could now afford it on Peter's money."

"Can you really get it back for Peter?"

"That is what I fully intend to do," the Marquess said in a voice of determination.

Athina got up from the sofa.

"Let us go and tell him that he need no longer be afraid and this is his home from now on."

She walked towards the door and the Marquess joined her.

"That is one problem solved," he said, "but you must not forget mine."

Athina smiled.

"Have you let the Queen know that you are engaged?"

"I have written to the Lord Chamberlain," the Marquess replied, "but of course these things take time and it would seem very strange if, immediately after my appointment, you throw me out as unwanted."

Athina laughed.

"I will not do that until you tell me it is impossible for the Queen to take back what she had already given you."

"Thank you on my behalf," the Marquess said, "but I think Peter would be very upset if you left here."

"Mrs. Beckwith and I are very comfortable," Athina said demurely.

"I do not know whether it is I or Mrs. Field who should be gratified by that remark!" the Marquess retorted.

They were both laughing as they hurried up to the Sitting-Room which had been allotted to Peter as his School-Room.

They knew he would be waiting, trembling and apprehensive, until they reached him.

*   *   *

The next day Athina felt as if the dark clouds had vanished from the sky.

Peter was in high spirits as they rode with the Marquess over the Estate and he showed them the improvements he was making.

It surprised him how much Athina knew about farming methods.

He learned that she not only had, as she had said, a number of breeding-mares at Murling, but also a pig-farm which was doing exceptionally well.

"That is something I had not thought of," he admitted. "You must take me over and show me your Estate. It is not very far to go."

"Not if we ride," Athina agreed. "But it takes far longer if we go by road."

"We will ride!" the Marquess said firmly.

"Please, may I come too?" Peter begged. "I would love to see Aunt Athina's horses and find out if they are as good as yours."

"They are not," Athina said, "but I love them just as they are."

She spoke a little defiantly, and the Marquess was about to answer, when Peter said:

"I worry about poor *Ladybird*. Do you think that Step-Papa is still beating her? Her back was all sores like mine."

"I will tell you what I will do," the Marquess said. "If your Stepfather is hard up, as I think he is, I will, if it is possible, buy *Ladybird* from him.

She will be your special horse."

"Oh . . . could you . . . would you really . . . do that?" Peter asked. "She is such a . . . lovely mare, and I do not . . . think anybody was . . . kind to her . . . except me."

"I promise I will try," the Marquess replied. "Then you can make her happy at Rock."

"I am happy," Peter said, "very, very happy! It is only when I think about *Ladybird* that I am sad."

"Leave it to me," the Marquess said.

Athina felt that no-one could be more kind or more understanding of the feelings of a small boy.

Now, as they went round the Estate, the Marquess explained to her why he had stayed away from Rock for so long.

Her Father had been wrong in thinking he had only wanted to enjoy himself in London.

He was feeling what any young man would—frustrated and offended because nobody would listen to him.

His Father would not even consider the improvements which he knew were necessary.

"We will go over to Murling first thing tomorrow morning," the Marquess said now.

"We will have luncheon there," Athina answered, "and perhaps you could send a groom to warn my servants to prepare a good meal."

She paused before she said:

"Mrs. Bell has been the Cook ever since I was a child, and although her food cannot rival that of your Chef, I hope you will find it enjoyable."

"I am sure I shall," the Marquess said, "and I

shall be very interested to see your home."

Athina thought it would be rather fun to show it to him.

It would not in any way compare with the magnificence of Rock.

It was, however, a very old house and very picturesque.

She thought the Marquess might find it interesting to compare the two Estates.

She was beginning to feel guilty that in staying at Rock she was neglecting her duties at home.

At the same time, she knew it would upset Peter if she left him.

The Marquess was quite right in thinking that not for a moment did anyone question that their engagement was anything but genuine.

She thought it amusing to be deceiving the Queen.

Her Majesty had been most unfair in insisting that the Marquess should be married or engaged before he could take up the post of Master of the Horse.

"What are you thinking about?" the Marquess asked unexpectedly.

"I was actually thinking that you will make a very good Master of the Horse, and since your Uncle, Lord Edward Rock, was not really a good horseman, I am sure there will be a great deal to be done to the Royal Stables."

"That is what I thought," the Marquess agreed with satisfaction, "and I intend to make the Queen's Stud outstanding."

Athina was quite certain that, as in everything else, he would succeed in his aims.

She knew he was in many ways an exceptional man.

"I shall be very glad of your advice about Murling," she said aloud. "I have put in many innovations since I have been running it, but when I saw yours, I realised how much more there is for me to do."

"I hope you will let me help you," the Marquess said simply.

"I should be very disappointed if you did not," Athina replied.

Peter went to bed after an early supper.

At dinner that night the Marquess had insisted that Athina and Mrs. Beckwith celebrate with him the victory which had been won over Lord Burnham.

They drank champagne, and as they sipped it, Athina asked:

"You are quite certain he has not a trump-card up his sleeve? Will he do something we have not thought of which will upset Peter?"

"I doubt it," the Marquess said. "I have already written to my Solicitors to tell them that he is to receive a considerable sum of money every year so long as he does not dispute my Guardianship and does not interfere with Peter in any way."

"That is marvellous!" Athina said.

"He needs the money," the Marquess said in a satisfied tone, "and if he troubles us in the future, we will simply stop the payments."

Athina looked at him with admiration in her eyes.

He thought it was certainly an improvement on the way she had looked at him when they first met.

*   *   *

The next morning Peter was in a state of excitement at the idea of going to Murling Park.

"You must show me all your horses, Aunt Athina," he said, "and I expect they will be thrilled to see you."

"I am sure they will," Athina agreed. "The names I have given them are Greek, like my own. You must tell them to Mrs. Beckwith, who will have a story about each of the gods and goddesses after whom they have been named."

"Mrs. Beckwith's stories are jolly good!" Peter approved. "She plays a game with me when we do Arithmetic, which makes it fun!"

Athina knew from her own experience what a clever teacher Mrs. Beckwith was.

She thought, as she had thought before, how fortunate Peter was to have her.

The one thing she could not teach him was riding.

"You are quite certain you do not want to come with us?" Athina asked her.

Mrs. Beckwith shook her head.

"I will come with you another day, when we go in the Chaise, or in His Lordship's Dog-cart," she replied.

"And I will come with you," Peter said. "I want to see the dogs running underneath it."

He had already made friends with the Marquess's Dalmatians.

Athina was looking forward to showing him her Spaniels.

She wondered if she could ask the Marquess if she could bring one back with her.

But she was afraid he might object to adding to the dogs that were already loose about the house.

The horses were waiting for them after breakfast.

Just as they went outside to mount them, Dawson came to tell the Marquess that one of the Farmers wanted to see him.

"There's been a spot of bother at his Farm, M'Lord," he said. "The roof's fallen in."

"I had better come to see him," the Marquess answered.

Athina and Peter were already mounted.

"You two go ahead," the Marquess said, "and I will catch up with you. I should not be long."

"We will not hurry," Athina replied. "I expect you know the way. It is through Monk's Wood."

"I will find you quite easily," the Marquess promised.

He went back into the house.

Athina and Peter rode out of the court-yard and down the drive towards the lake.

They crossed over the ancient bridge which spanned it.

Then they rode under the trees in the Park.

They disturbed the deer who moved away, but

not very fast because they were almost tame.

At the far end of the Park was Monk's Wood.

There was a ride through it which led eventually to the Murling Estate.

Athina remembered that when she was a small girl there had been at one time a heated argument between her Father and the late Marquess.

The Earl had complained to the Marquess that his guests who shot by Monk's Wood were killing *his* pheasants.

The Marquess, on the other hand, asserted that when the Earl shot near that particular boundary, it was the Rock pheasants that were being killed.

It was an argument that had no ending.

It was now a warm, sunny day and the woods looked very beautiful.

The leaves of the trees were still the pale green of Spring.

The bluebells were over, but there were still some wild daffodils left to give a touch of gold.

Peeping from among their leaves were purple and white violets.

The path narrowed, and Athina led the way with Peter following.

There was still no sign of the Marquess, and she therefore rode slowly.

She wanted to see the expression on his face when he first saw Murling Park.

It was a low-built house with diamond-paned windows.

It had the strange thick, twisting chimneys of the Elizabethan era.

Everybody when they first saw it exclaimed at how romantic it looked.

She wondered what adjective the Marquess would use.

They reached the centre of the wood.

Here the ride was a little wider and Athina pulled in her horse.

"I wonder what is keeping your Uncle?" she asked.

"He will soon catch up with us if he rides very fast," Peter replied.

"I cannot hear him coming," Athina said a little anxiously.

Then, as she glanced round, she said:

"Look, Peter! There is a poor little bird that must have just fallen out of the nest, or been thrown out by a cuckoo."

Peter bent forward to look to where Athina was pointing.

There, sure enough, were two little baby birds lying on the ground with their beaks open.

He bent farther so that he could have a closer look.

It saved his life.

There was an explosion of gunfire and a bullet buried itself in the tree in front of him.

Athina gave a gasp and Peter exclaimed:

"What was that?"

"Ride! Ride quickly! Go, go!" she ordered.

Obediently he passed her.

She pulled her horse in behind him to shelter him from any further danger.

Peter rode at a tremendous pace through the wood.

Athina managed to keep up with him.

As they came to the end of the trees and rode out into an open field, Peter reined in his horse.

"Somebody . . . shot at . . . me . . . Aunt Athina!" he exclaimed.

Before Athina could answer, she saw, to her relief, the Marquess.

He must have passed through the woods a little higher up.

He was coming down the field at a sharp trot.

"Tell your Uncle what happened," she said.

Peter obediently rode towards him.

As he did so, Athina knew that they had been too optimistic in thinking they had won the battle.

Lord Burnham, as she had thought from the very first, would be a relentless enemy.

chapter six

PETER galloped up to the Marquess.

"Someone shot at me, Uncle Denzil," he shouted, "the bullet went straight past my head!"

The Marquess stared at him, then he said:

"Come on, let us get away from here."

He started to ride across the field in the direction of the Murling Estate.

Seeing what they were doing, Athina followed them.

They went across another field.

Only when they reached the trees which bordered the drive of her house did the Marquess pull in his horse.

"I will tell you what happened," Athina said as she joined them. "We were riding through the wood, slowly because we were waiting for you to catch up with us. Then we stopped to hear if you were coming and I saw a bird that had fallen out of its nest."

"There were two, there were two!" Peter interposed.

"There were two," Athina corrected herself. "Peter bent forward to look at them. As he did so, a shot rang out and the bullet buried itself in a tree, passing just where Peter's head would . . . have . . . been."

She saw the Marquess's lips tighten.

As her voice faltered, he realised she was very pale and it had obviously been a shock.

He put out his hand.

Athina had taken off her glove to press her hand to her face. Instead, she put it into his.

She felt that the strength of his fingers was very comforting.

"Are you all right?" he asked.

"Yes," she answered. "I . . . I am all . . . right."

She did not sound very certain about it.

The Marquess looked at her searchingly as he said:

"Let us go on up to your house. I do not imagine there is anything we can do. The man who fired at Peter will have made a quick getaway."

As he spoke, Athina saw her game-keeper coming down the drive with two dogs at his heels.

She took her hand from the Marquess's and said:

"There is Wilkins, my game-keeper."

The Marquess rode up to the man, and as he touched his forelock said to him:

"There is, we think, a poacher in Monk's Wood. As I cannot get hold of any of my keepers in a hurry, I would be grateful if you would go and see what is happening. Her Ladyship heard a shot as she was coming here."

"Oi'll go at once, M'Lord," Wilkins answered. "They poachers be everywhere, an' they does a lot o' damage t'the young birds!"

"I know that only too well," the Marquess replied.

The game-keeper walked away and his dogs followed him.

When he was out of ear-shot, the Marquess said:

"I doubt if he will find anybody there. They would not stay to be caught."

"Do you think it was Step-Papa who was trying to . . . kill me?" Peter asked.

"It was probably just a poacher, as I said," the Marquess replied, "shooting the pigeons."

He spoke casually.

Athina was aware he was trying to prevent Peter from being frightened.

She knew that she herself was terrified.

How was it possible in the quiet of the country that somebody could be lurking on the Marquess's land, waiting to murder Peter?

It could be Lord Burnham himself.

But more likely it was someone he had hired to do his dirty work for him.

"What are we . . . to do? What . . . are we to . . . do?" she asked herself as they rode on up the drive.

The Marquess was looking at Murling Park with great interest, and as they neared it he said:

"I had forgotten, for I have not been here since I was about twelve, how beautiful your house is."

"I hoped you would think so," Athina answered.

"There is nothing more attractive," the Marquess went on, "than the pink of Elizabethan bricks when they have been mellowed by the centuries."

Athina managed to smile.

He was right, and he was appreciating her home.

There were two grooms waiting to take their horses.

As they walked up to the front-door, an ancient Butler opened it.

Then there was the patter of feet as three small Spaniels came bursting out.

They jumped up at Athina, barking excitedly because she had come home.

As she bent to pat them, Peter did the same.

"They are very pleased to see you, Aunt Athina," he shouted above the noise the dogs were making.

Athina was making a particular fuss of one outstandingly good-looking Spaniel.

"This is *Flash*," she said to Peter. "I have had him ever since he was born. He goes everywhere with me when I am at home."

"He must have missed you while you were at Rock," Peter remarked.

"You can see he did," Athina replied.

Flash was trying in every way he knew to tell her how glad he was she was back.

The Marquess was watching.

As she gave the Spaniel a final pat and rose to her feet, he said:

"I can see I have been very remiss in not including *Flash* among my guests."

Athina's eyes lit up.

"Do you really mean that I can bring him to Rock? I had thought of asking you, but I was afraid it would be an imposition."

Before the Marquess could reply, Peter chimed in:

"Oh, please, Uncle Denzil, let Aunt Athina have *Flash* to stay with us. I will look after him and he can sleep in my room."

Athina thought this was a good idea, and *Flash* would certainly help to protect him.

If by any chance an intruder entered Peter's bedroom, she knew that *Flash* would bark and very likely attack him.

There was no need to express in words what she was thinking.

As she looked at the Marquess, she was aware that he thought the same.

"We will take *Flash* back with us," he said.

Athina then took him over the house.

She felt touched that he appreciated the low ceilings, the diamond-paned windows, and the big open fireplaces.

It was all so very different from his own house.

Peter was delighted with everything he saw.

When they sat down to luncheon, she thought with satisfaction that Mrs. Bell had excelled herself.

She had cooked dishes which they all enjoyed.

When luncheon was over, they went into the garden.

Peter started throwing a ball for *Flash* and the other dogs.

Athina and the Marquess sat down on a wooden seat in the rose-garden.

It was the first time they had been alone together without Peter, and Athina asked:

"What are you going to do about the man in the wood?"

"There is really nothing I can do," the Marquess answered. "I am quite certain your game-keeper will find nothing by the time he gets there."

"But . . . he will . . . try again," Athina faltered.

"I am aware of that," the Marquess said, "but I can hardly confine Peter to the house, or send him out only under armed guard."

Athina made a helpless little gesture with her hands.

"I am . . . frightened," she said, "very . . . very . . . frightened!"

"I understand that," the Marquess said, "and we can only pray that we will be protected."

She was so surprised at what he said that she looked at him questioningly.

"If you think about it," he said quietly, "Fate, or Peter's Guardian Angel, brought you into his life at a moment when, if I am not mistaken, Burnham was intent on murdering him."

"How can a man who is in the House of Lords and has held Government posts, be prepared actually to commit murder?" Athina asked.

"His financial position must be even worse than I thought," the Marquess replied. "I am convinced now that he married my sister entirely for her money, even though he was genuinely attracted by her."

Athina made no comment.

The Marquess went on as if he were puzzling it out for himself:

"I was, in fact, very surprised when she married again. She was broken-hearted at the death of Gerald Naver. He was a charming and delightful person whom everybody loved."

"Then why did she marry so soon after he died?" Athina asked.

"I suppose the truth was that she did not care what happened to her," the Marquess replied, "and when Burnham wooed her so ardently, she thought it would be good for Peter to have another Father."

"I can understand . . . that," Athina said slowly.

"As we now know, it was disastrous," the Marquess went on, "and when Burnham knew Louise was dying, he was determined to get all the money for himself."

"Which is . . . what he . . . wants . . . now," Athina murmured.

"As I told you, I have already arranged for him to be offered a very considerable annual income," the Marquess said, "but I gather from what happened this afternoon, that it is not enough."

There was a note of anger in his voice as he spoke.

Athina looked at the squareness of his chin and the expression in his eyes.

She thought he was like a Knight going into battle against the Powers of Darkness.

Then she thought it was a strange way to be thinking of the Marquess, whom at first she had so strongly disliked and disapproved of.

Yet how could she disapprove of him now, when he was fighting so determinedly for Peter's life?

Peter came running back to them.

"*Flash* is quicker than all the other dogs! He always gets the ball first!"

"That is why I called him *Flash*," Athina answered. "Even as a puppy he was very quick-witted and instantly gobbled up his dinner quicker than the rest."

Peter laughed.

"That is what Uncle Denzil likes me to do. I am getting fat. My riding-breeches already are getting too tight round my waist."

"You must tell Mrs. Field," Athina said. "I am sure she will have another pair a little bigger which at one time belonged to your Uncle."

"I will tell her," Peter said, "but I think in about a week I will want a bigger pair than that!"

They laughed and Peter ran off again to play with the dogs.

Athina suddenly felt afraid that within a week or so he might not be there.

She turned to the Marquess.

"What can . . . we do? Or, rather, what can . . . *you* do?" she asked.

"That is what I am trying to puzzle out," he replied, "and I think now we should go back to Rock. We will go by a roundabout way which will take much longer than going through Monk's Wood."

Athina shivered.

She could still hear the sound of the shot as the bullet buried itself in the tree behind Peter.

She did not speak, but the Marquess knew what she was thinking.

"Trust me," he said. "At the same time, Peter must never be left alone."

"No, of course not," Athina agreed.

The horses were brought round to the front.

Athina said good-bye to Mrs. Bell and thanked her for the luncheon.

She then told Upton, the old Butler, to look after everything.

"Will Your Ladyship be acoming back soon?" he asked.

"I am not sure, Upton," she replied. "But I know everything will be safe in your capable hands, and His Lordship may wish to come over again in a day or so."

Because of what had happened in the wood, they had not gone to see her mares or the pigs as she had intended.

She knew the Marquess felt the same as she did.

If they strayed too far from the house, it would be easy for a gunman to take another shot at Peter.

They mounted their horses.

The Marquess moved off quickly, leading them through the stables instead of down the drive.

He rode away from the house in a different direction from what he would have taken if they were returning straight to Rock.

Peter was very happy riding behind his Uncle on a very well-bred horse.

He did not, therefore, seem to notice that they

were returning to Rock by a different route.

He chattered about the birds, the sheep, and the cattle they passed.

He kept an eye on *Flash*, who was running behind them.

It was not until they came in sight of Rock that he said:

"That was a long way home, Uncle Denzil! But it was a scrumptious ride!"

"I am glad you enjoyed it," the Marquess said, "and I think we will ride straight into the stables instead of dismounting at the front-door as we usually do."

Peter made no comment.

Athina knew that the Marquess was avoiding the open court-yard at the front of the house.

If anyone was watching for them, it was where they would expect them to dismount.

They rode into the stables, where a number of grooms and stable-lads were moving about.

Athina was not surprised when the Marquess took them into the house by the kitchen door.

He made the excuse that he wanted to show Peter the Dairy.

There were huge bowls of milk left on marble slabs every night so that there would be plenty of cream in the morning.

Peter was fascinated by it.

Athina, however, knew that the servants were surprised to see the Marquess in a part of Rock he did not usually visit.

They reached the hall and the main staircase.

Peter ran up it, calling *Flash* so that he could show the dog to Mrs. Beckwith.

She was sitting in an armchair and, as Athina had expected, reading a book.

As Peter rushed in, he told her first about *Flash* and how he had come to stay with them.

Then he remembered to tell her that a shot had been fired at him.

When he did so, he said:

"It was very . . . frightening, but Aunt Athina told me to ride away quickly, and I galloped out of the Wood as fast as I could go. Then I saw Uncle Denzil."

"It all sounds horrifying to me," Mrs. Beckwith exclaimed, "but lots of Kings and Queens have been shot at! Tomorrow we will find some books about them and you will see that they were as brave as you were."

"That will be fun!" Peter smiled.

He ran down the corridor to his bedroom to change from his riding-breeches.

Mrs. Beckwith said to Athina:

"How can this happen in England, of all places? And here in the country, where everything is so peaceful!"

"That is what I have been asking," Athina replied, "and if it had not been for the birds, Peter would now be dead!"

Mrs. Beckwith put a hand on her arm.

"I am sure the Marquess will do something about that man," she said. "This cannot go on!"

"That is exactly what I have been saying," Athina

answered, "but how can we know when he will strike again?"

She felt the tears come into her eyes and hurried to her own room to change.

They came downstairs for tea in the Drawing-Room.

Athina, by this time, felt more composed and knew it was a mistake to keep talking about what had happened.

Instead, when Mrs. Beckwith joined them, they talked about Murling.

"It is reputed that Queen Elizabeth once slept there," Athina remarked.

"The number of houses supposed to have put her up for the night are so many," the Marquess said sarcastically, "that I can only think Her Majesty never ceased travelling around her Kingdom, and found London itself very boring."

"That is the opposite of what you thought," Athina said teasingly. "When I first heard about you from my Father, he told me he had no use for young 'toffs' who wanted only to enjoy themselves with beautiful women in London and were bored in the country."

The Marquess laughed.

"Was that really my reputation?"

"It was much worse than that," Athina went on, "but I am too polite to mention it!"

The Marquess was about to expostulate when Peter said:

"I love being in the country. I want just to live here and ride Uncle Denzil's horses. And I want dozens and dozens of dogs like *Flash*."

"Not all in the house, I hope!" the Marquess said quickly. "My carpets are very valuable."

"I would train them so that they never did anything naughty," Peter promised.

"That would definitely be a step in the right direction," the Marquess admitted.

Flash was very content to play with Peter.

They scrambled about on the floor.

Watching them, Athina thought it was difficult to recognise the pale, frightened, half-starved little boy sobbing miserably for his Mother when she first met him.

When later they sat talking, she thought anyone who saw them would think they were just an ordinary Family with no great problems to solve.

Certainly not with a murderer worrying them.

"Lord Burnham should be hanged!" she said to herself.

She shied away from the thought that she and the Marquess might be worrying over their own son.

Whether their conversation took place in a cottage or in the magnificence of Rock, it would be just the same.

'The sooner Lord Burnham is out of our lives and I can go home, the better,' she decided.

Because she was always honest with herself, she knew that for the moment, at any rate, she would rather be at Rock alone with the Marquess.

Peter begged that he might have dinner with them.

The Marquess agreed, mainly, Athina thought,

because he would then be able to keep his eye on him.

While he was with them, nobody had to worry about what was happening to him.

As Athina put on one of her pretty gowns she had bought to wear in London, she thought how extraordinary the Marquess was.

He usually had his friends staying with him at Rock, she supposed.

Now he was apparently content to have just herself and Mrs. Beckwith there.

Actually she herself should be in London at this moment, preparing to be presented at Buckingham Palace.

She would be counting her invitations to all the Balls as they arrived every morning.

She had written a letter which was almost truthful to the relation with whom she had arranged to stay.

She had explained that she had problems at Murling and could not leave.

She added:

It may be a question of a week, or perhaps only days, and by now you may have seen the announcement in the Gazette *that I am engaged to the Marquess of Rockingdale.*

I know Papa would be pleased, as our Estates march with each other.

As soon as I come to London you will, of course, meet him, and I am sure you will find him delightful. . . .

She wrote more or less the same letter to her other relatives, making the same excuse for not coming to London immediately.

She was sure they would think it extraordinary when her coming-out had all been arranged.

Then she thought:

'They will expect me to attend the first Drawing-Room, and then another after I am married.'

Yet it was impossible for her to leave Peter just now.

Besides, if she and the Marquess took Peter to London with them, it would be easier for him to have an unfortunate "accident" of some sort there.

After dinner, when Mrs. Beckwith had taken Peter up to bed, Athina and the Marquess were left alone.

It was then she said:

"I am feeling very guilty. I am sure you ought to be in London enjoying the Season, just as I should be. And yet, I am afraid of going there with Peter in case it is even more dangerous for him to be there."

"It is dangerous wherever he goes," the Marquess said, "but once I catch Burnham red-handed, I can threaten him so that he will be too frightened to try again."

"How could you do that?" Athina asked.

"He is afraid of a scandal, and I should, of course, accuse him of attempted murder."

Athina gave a little cry.

"Can . . . you do . . . that?"

"If I catch him in the act," the Marquess said.

"Alternatively I can force him to live abroad and give him enough money to do so."

"That would be a better solution," Athina said. "Oh, please . . . please . . . let us hope that . . . we do not have to . . . wait too . . . long."

"Are you already so bored with being here with me?" the Marquess asked unexpectedly.

"No, of course not," Athina replied quickly, "but I feel very guilty when I think of how boring it must be for you."

"I have not said I am bored," the Marquess assured her. "In fact, although I agree with you that the situation is frightening, I have never felt more alert and purposeful. I am determined to rid us of this menace which is certainly very bad for Peter as well as for you."

"I do not . . . matter," Athina replied. "But he is such a . . . dear little boy, and . . . one day he will . . . have to go to . . . School."

"I can only hope to God that I shall have dealt with Burnham long before that!" the Marquess said sharply.

Athina thought it had been a tactless thing for her to say.

It implied that the Marquess would have to continue with his protection of Peter rather than live his own life.

She wondered how many lovely ladies were finding it extraordinary that he continued to stay in the country, where they could not see him.

She thought how dull it must be for him to have

only her and Mrs. Beckwith to talk to.

In London there had been the dazzling Beauties who frequented Marlborough House.

"If we are talking about people missing London," the Marquess said, "what about you? I understand from Mrs. Beckwith that you expected to be presented at the first Drawing-Room and should by now be counting your invitations to Balls."

It was something Athina had herself been thinking in identical words, and she answered quickly:

"Nothing matters! Nothing and nobody except Peter! Anyway, as I am a country girl, I prefer being here to staying in London."

"That is nonsense!" the Marquess said argumentatively. "You know perfectly well it is the dream of every young woman to be the 'Belle of the Ball,' the 'Beauty of the Season,' and have a dozen young men asking for her hand in marriage!"

Athina laughed.

"I think it far more likely," she said, "that I shall be joining the rows of *débutantes* whom, I am told, smart gentlemen like yourself ignore as if they had the plague!"

The Marquess laughed.

"I must admit I do not know any *débutantes*, nor have I ever even spoken to one! But they do exist, and I suppose they have their place in the Social World."

"Most men have to marry some time," Athina said, "and one day when all this is over you will inevitably find yourself walking down the aisle with a ravishing *débutante* who is the 'Beauty of the Season.' "

"That is exactly what I have always been afraid of," the Marquess replied, "and I suppose it is what will happen to me if the Queen has her way."

He spoke aggressively, and there was silence until Athina said:

"When we break off our engagement, you do not think your position as Master of the Horse will be taken away from you?"

"It is what the Queen might want to do," the Marquess said in a serious tone. "At the same time, if I prove myself, as I intend to be really good at my job, it will be difficult for her to find a plausible excuse for dismissing me."

"I am glad about that," Athina said.

"And of course while we are talking about it," the Marquess said, "if the Man of your Dreams comes down the chimney, or you meet him unexpectedly, then you must tell me immediately and we will put the wheels in motion to set you free."

"Meanwhile you are quite safe," Athina said. "Unless you have invited a number of your friends to stay, I am not likely to meet any eligible bachelors."

"Is that what you want?" the Marquess enquired.

"You know it is not!" Athina replied. "I have already told you that I have no wish to be married, and I would never marry unless I were very much . . . in love."

"And how will you know if that is what you are feeling?" the Marquess asked.

She looked at him in a rather startled fashion.

"I have never thought of that," she replied, "but I suppose one does know when one is in love. One must feel different, or is that just a lot of nonsense invented by the Poets?"

The Marquess smiled.

"I promise you, Athina, that when you are in love, you will be very much aware of it."

There was silence for a moment.

Then she asked:

"Is it a very . . . very . . . wonderful feeling?"

"So I have always been told," the Marquess replied.

She looked at him in astonishment.

"You have always been *told?*" she repeated. "But surely you must have been in love dozens of times?"

The Marquess seemed for the moment at a loss for words.

Then he said:

"Real love, which is what you had in mind, as perhaps nonsense the Poets write about, is not the same as what passes for love in the Social World. It is something very different."

"How is that . . . possible?" Athina asked.

"Men and women have been physically attracted to each other since the beginning of creation," the Marquess said, "which is right and natural."

He paused as if he were choosing his words before he went on:

"But such attraction is something very different from what we are talking about, and which we are both very ignorant of at the moment."

"How is it different?" Athina asked.

She was enthralled by this conversation.

It was something she had never talked about with anyone before.

Her Father had once said when she had asked him:

"When I was very young I fell very much in love with a beautiful girl, but she married somebody else."

"Were you very unhappy, Papa?" Athina had asked.

"Because I was young and impetuous," her Father replied, "I felt suicidal. But eventually there were other women who, although I never felt the same again for them, made me almost forget what I had suffered."

It was unlike her Father to be so communicative about his past.

After that he had never referred to it again.

She had often wondered if that was why he had never really got on with her Mother.

Her Mother too had been in love.

She had said that her heart had been broken when she could not marry the man she called William.

The Marquess was looking at Athina while she was thinking, and after a moment he said:

"You are very lovely, Athina, and altogether worthy of your name. I can promise you that when you get to London, there will be many men who will lay their hearts at your feet!"

"But . . . supposing," Athina asked in a small

voice, "my . . . heart does not . . . respond?"

"If you are wise," the Marquess advised, "you will stick to your guns and refuse to marry until the right man comes along."

"That is what I want to do," Athina said quietly.

"Let me assure you that he will come along," the Marquess said, "and then you will instinctively know what love is, and that it is exactly what you have dreamt about."

Athina thought this really told her very little of what she wanted to know.

They then talked of other things and laughed a lot.

Yet she was still thinking of love when she went up to bed.

She went into Peter's room and saw that he was fast asleep.

The Marquess had arranged that Peter slept in the room next to hers.

His Master Suite was just a little farther down the corridor.

Mrs. Beckwith was some distance away, next to a delightful room which the Marquess had allotted to Peter as a School-Room.

Athina was aware that if things had been normal, he would have been put on the Nurseries floor.

As she went to her own room she thought it would be impossible for anyone to get at him from outside the house.

When she had looked into Peter's room she had seen *Flash* curled up at the bottom of his bed.

He did not jump up and go to her as he usually did.

Instead, he just wagged his tail.

She knew that with the instinct of an intelligent dog he understood that he was there to guard Peter.

She patted him gently, looking at Peter as he slept.

She then went from the room, carrying the candle with which she had lighted her way upstairs.

The Marquess had installed electric light in most of the bedrooms.

But because it was traditional, every guest was handed a candle by a footman before they went up to bed.

It was something that had always been done at Murling Park too, and her Father insisted on it.

Athina knew she would miss it if it were superseded by modern appliances.

In her own room she put the candle down by her bed and left it burning.

There was no doubt in this magnificent State Room with its four-poster bed that candlelight was far more romantic.

There was a small candelabrum holding three lighted candles on her dressing-table.

She therefore ignored the new light-switch beside the door and undressed by candlelight.

She had told the maid she would not need her.

She was thinking now of the strange conversation she had with the Marquess about love.

Never had she expected him to speak like that, or to admit what he was looking for.

It was not what was accepted by the Smart Set who centred round the Prince of Wales.

"Supposing I never find it?" Athina asked as she had put on her nightgown.

Then she told herself there was so much beauty and romance in the world.

She could not be the only person to be left out.

She longed to find the love that was very beautiful, very desirable, and very inspiring.

She went to the window to pull back the curtains.

There was a cloud over the moon, and the lake was not turned to silver as it had been on other nights.

The Park was dark.

Unable to find in it the message she was seeking, she pulled the curtains to again.

Blowing out the candles on her dressing-table, she got into bed.

She was wondering whether she should pray that one day she would find love.

It was something she had never done before.

Yet now, as she thought about what the Marquess had said, she had the strange feeling it was something he too was praying he would find.

Not on his knees, not in actual words, but in his heart.

It seemed to her very surprising it had eluded him.

"He is a very strange man," she told herself, "and utterly different from what I expected."

chapter seven

ATHINA did not fall asleep at once.

She was going over in her mind everything that had happened.

She felt as if they were all standing on the edge of a precipice.

Just one puff of wind would send them hurtling down into dreadful depths from which they would never escape.

"What shall . . . we do? What can . . . we do?"

The very walls were repeating the words in her mind.

Then at last she slept.

She was dreaming that she was galloping with the Marquess over a field to which there was no end.

They galloped and galloped, side by side.

Then she heard a little voice say: "Aunt . . . Athina! I . . . want . . . you!"

Peter was standing by her bed.

He had left the door open and the light coming from the sconces in the corridor silhouetted his head.

"Peter!" Athina exclaimed, "What is the matter?"

"I was . . . dreaming . . . of Mum . . . ma," Peter said in a hesitating voice, "and she . . . told me to . . . get up. I got up . . . Aunt Athina . . . and when I . . . looked out of the window . . . I saw Step-Papa—I am . . . sure it . . . was him—riding up . . . the drive on . . . a horse."

Knowing how dark it was outside, Athina thought this was unlikely and part of his dream, and he really could have seen nothing.

Yet she knew he was genuinely frightened.

"Climb into bed with me, and you can tell me what your Mother said and if you could see her clearly. It must have been very exciting for you."

Peter scrambled onto the bed and slipped between the sheets.

"Now . . . I feel . . . safe," he said.

"You are safe here," Athina assured him, "and no-one will harm you."

She drew him close to her and kissed him.

As she did so, she realised he was still half-asleep.

"Shut your eyes," she said softly, "and think about your Mama. I am sure she is near you and is protecting you."

Peter snuggled down against the pillows and Athina got out of bed.

By the light coming through the door she could see her negligee on a chair.

She put it on.

She then went to the window to discover if it

was in fact possible that he could have seen Lord Burnham coming up the drive.

She pulled the curtain a little way to one side and looked out.

It was very dark, with the moon still hidden behind a thick bank of cloud.

The stars were barely reflected in the lake.

As far as she could see, the drive with its oak trees was empty.

She could only just see the outline of the ancient bridge which spanned the lake.

Her eyes travelled from the bridge to a thick cluster of shrubs.

They hid from view the stable-buildings at one side of the house.

She stared at them.

Her eyes grew more accustomed to the darkness.

She thought, although it might have been part of her imagination, that she saw a movement in the shrubs.

She could not be certain, although she leaned out of the window, trying to see more clearly.

There was not a breath of wind and everything was absolutely still.

Then she thought, although she still could not be sure, that there really was some movement among the shrubs.

She felt fear streak through her as if it were lightning.

Turning from the window, she moved across the room towards the bed.

Peter was breathing rhythmically and there was no doubt he was fast asleep.

She looked at him for a moment.

Then she went out into the corridor, shutting the door behind her.

She ran the short distance to the Marquess's bedroom.

The outer door opened into a small hall and there was another door into the bedroom itself.

She did not knock, she just walked in.

As she did so, she realised that the room was not in darkness.

There was a light by the bed.

A huge four-poster bed hung with red velvet had the family Coat of Arms embroidered above the headboard.

The Marquess was propped up on several pillows.

He had obviously been reading a book which lay open in front of him.

While reading he had fallen asleep.

His eyes were shut and his head was against the pillows behind him.

Frightened though she was, Athina was aware that he looked exceedingly handsome.

Just for a moment she hesitated as to whether she should wake him.

Then she remembered that Peter said he had been woken by his Mother.

She knew that wherever she might be, Lady Louise was trying to protect her son.

Athina moved closer and touched the Marquess's hand which lay on the book.

"Wake up!" she said urgently. "Wake up!"

The Marquess, having once been a soldier, was instantly alert.

"Athina!" he exclaimed. "What is it?"

"I think, but it may be just my imagination," Athina explained, "that there is ... somebody ... moving about ... in the shrubs at the side of the court-yard."

The Marquess did not argue; he quickly got out of bed.

Going to a chair on which his Valet had left a long dark robe, he put it on.

"Is Peter asleep?" he asked.

"He came to me," Athina answered, "saying that he had dreamt of his Mother, who had told him to get up. When he looked out of the window he thought he saw his Stepfather riding up the drive."

She saw the surprise on the Marquess's face and added quickly:

"He was half-asleep and it was so dark that I did not think he could really have seen anything ... but I do think that something is ... moving in the ... shrubs."

As she spoke, she was afraid the Marquess would think she was just being hysterical.

The movement, if she had seen it, had been very slight.

At the same time, she was frightened.

If Lord Burnham did get into the house, he might try to kill Peter before they were aware he was there.

The Marquess buttoned up his robe, then went to the chest of drawers.

Athina saw that on the top of it there was lying both a rifle and a revolver.

The Marquess picked up the revolver first and held it out to her.

"Carry this," he said, "and be careful. It is loaded."

He then picked up the rifle.

"I was thinking, before I fell asleep," he said, "that although it is difficult to believe, Burnham undoubtedly has somebody in this house who is an informer. Somebody must have told him where we were going today."

Athina looked startled.

"Do . . . you mean . . . a spy?" she questioned.

"It may be some half-witted scullion or an odd-job man who will accept money, having no idea of the consequences of what he was doing."

The Marquess almost snapped the words at her.

Then, picking up the rifle, he walked towards the door.

"Peter is in my bed," she said.

"I have no wish for the boy to be frightened," the Marquess replied. "What we have to find out is where Burnham intends to enter the house."

He did not say any more, but opened the door into the passage.

Athina followed him.

They went along the corridor, but not towards the main staircase which led to the Hall.

Instead, they went to what she knew was a secondary staircase and was seldom used.

There was just enough light in the corridor and at the foot of the stairs for them to see their way.

They reached the Ground Floor.

The Marquess went quickly to the first of the rooms facing onto the court-yard and opened the door.

For a moment Athina did not know what he was looking for.

Then, as he shut the door and went on to the next, she understood.

When the Adam brothers had practically rebuilt the house in about 1760 they had put on a new facade.

It made Rock look extremely impressive and very beautiful.

The Ground Floor had tall Georgian windows rising from only a few feet above ground level.

In consequence, for safety, they had strong wooden shutters inside.

These were closed at night by the footman.

The Marquess hurried from room to room.

Athina knew that what he expected to find was that Lord Burnham's accomplice had left the shutters open in one room.

In which case, if the window was not fastened, he had only to push it up.

He could then enter the room without any difficulty.

The Marquess opened door after door.

Athina began to think he was mistaken and Lord Burnham was planning to enter the house by some other means.

At last in a Sitting-Room next to the Library the Marquess found what he was seeking.

As he opened the door, Athina could see at first glance a glimpse of shining glass.

This meant that the shutters were open.

The Marquess went into the room.

When Athina followed him he did not walk towards the window.

Instead, he moved to one side and stood behind an armchair.

Now Athina could see that the window was already raised.

There was just room enough for a man to put his leg over the sill and climb in.

She was wondering who among the Marquess's servants could have behaved so treacherously.

She hoped it was not someone who had been at Rock for a long time.

She knew she must not speak or move.

She was aware that the Marquess was standing motionless with his rifle at the ready.

He was staring intently at the window.

There was no sound from outside.

Athina began to wonder if perhaps Lord Burnham had not, in fact, come down the drive as Peter dreamed he had.

Perhaps he had changed his mind and gone away again.

As her eyes became more accustomed to the darkness, she could see the stars.

The clouds were moving away from the moon.

The night air coming into the room was cool.

Then there was a sound.

It was only very faint, but unmistakably a sound in the court-yard.

Athina strained her ears to hear.

Then the sound came again, this time a little louder.

She was aware that the Marquess had drawn in his breath.

Although he had not moved, she knew he had heard, as she had, the sounds outside.

Now they came nearer and nearer still.

Somebody was moving stealthily and with covered shoes over the gravel.

Before she had expected it, so that she almost gave a scream, there was a large dark figure in front of the window.

It was undoubtedly Lord Burnham and he was wearing black.

It made him appear even more menacing.

There was a hood of some sort pulled over his head.

She thought too, although she could not see clearly, that he wore a mask.

Now Athina saw that he held something white in his hand.

He looked up at the window as if he were appraising it.

Then, putting the hand which held whatever it was that was white inside, he put his leg over the sill.

As he did so, there was a sudden ominous growl and then a sharp bark.

Flash rushed from behind Athina towards the window.

She had had no idea that he had left Peter and followed her and the Marquess downstairs.

He must have, in fact, left her room when she did.

Now he was barking furiously at Lord Burnham.

He threw his leg back sharply, dropping inside the room whatever it was he carried.

He staggered for a second outside the window.

Then, as *Flash* stood up against the sill, barking, Athina heard him hurrying away.

He was no longer treading softly as he went, but half-running, half-stumbling.

The Marquess moved quickly to the window and leant out, watching Lord Burnham make for the shrubbery.

Athina bent down to pick up what he had dropped.

It appeared, when she looked at it, to be a white linen face-towel.

Then she was aware that there was something thicker inside it.

As she bent her head to inspect it, she noticed a strange smell.

Before she could understand what it meant, the Marquess said in a low voice:

"Put it down! He has saturated it with chloroform. It would have rendered Peter unconscious, then, I imagine, he would have suffocated him with a pillow."

Athina gave a cry of horror.

She dropped the towel as the Marquess had told her to do.

Then she bent forward to look out of the window.

Lord Burnham was obviously finding it difficult to get back to where he had left his horse.

There was a delay of several minutes before he rode out from the shrubbery and proceeded towards the bridge.

As he did so, Athina was suddenly aware that the Marquess had gone down on one knee.

He was aiming his rifle at Lord Burnham.

It flashed through her mind that it would be very dangerous for him to shoot Lord Burnham.

Although he was an intruder and disguised, he was his brother-in-law.

It would undoubtedly cause a tremendous scandal.

The Marquess would be involved in a Court case and might even be convicted of man-slaughter.

She wanted to beg him not to do it.

And yet, even as she parted her lips to speak, she found it impossible to do so.

Lord Burnham had now reached the narrow bridge.

As he did so, the cloud that had obscured the moon moved away completely.

The moonlight shone dazzlingly on the lake.

It lit the ancient bridge and the man in the dark clothing approaching it on horseback.

"Do not shoo—!" Athina started to cry.

Then, to her surprise, she realised that the Marquess was pointing the rifle not at Lord Burnham, but at the bridge itself.

It had been built in Elizabethan times and was made of bricks which had mellowed with age.

At each end of the bridge stood a small statue.

With the passing of the years they had become somewhat worn and battered.

Now it was difficult to tell what they had originally represented.

The Marquess's Father had always refused to have them renewed or even repaired.

The Marquess was now aiming at the statue at the far end of the bridge.

Athina was puzzled by what he was doing.

She was aware that on the parapet of the bridge itself there were a number of birds.

There were ducks and moorhens perched there for the night.

She remembered vaguely having noticed them before when she looked out of the window.

Now, as Lord Burnham's horse stepped onto the bridge, the Marquess took careful aim.

He fired at the statue beyond where the birds were roosting.

The explosion and the shattering of the stone caused them to fly squawking with fear and resentment across the bridge and onto the bank on the other side.

The horse, frightened by the sudden sound and the movement of the birds, reared.

Lord Burnham, who was obviously somewhat insecure in the saddle, was thrown.

He landed on the parapet of the bridge, where he lay sprawled for a second.

Then, because he was too heavy and too fuddled with drink to save himself, he slipped slowly backwards into the lake.

The last Athina saw of him before he disappeared were his polished riding-boots shining in the moonlight.

His horse bolted into the Park, its stirrups jangling as it vanished amongst the trees.

Athina watched as if spellbound, unable to move or make any sound.

The Marquess put down the rifle and rose to his feet.

"That is the end," he said with satisfaction. "The water is very deep there, and anyway, he was in no condition to swim."

He spoke like a man who had found the answer to a problem which had threatened to defeat him.

It was then that Athina gave a gasp.

The horror of all she had witnessed made her feel as if she were going to faint.

Hardly knowing what she was doing, she moved towards the Marquess.

As he put his arms around her, she hid her face against his shoulder.

Without even realising that she was crying, the tears were running down her cheeks.

The Marquess held her close against him.

Then he said:

"It is all right, my Darling! It is all over, and Peter is safe."

Startled at the way he addressed her, Athina raised her head to look up at him.

The moonlight coming through the window shone in her eyes, still wide and frightened.

Tears glistened on her cheeks, and for a moment the Marquess just looked down at her.

Then he bent his head and his lips found hers.

Athina could not believe it was happening.

As the Marquess's mouth held hers captive, she felt as if the stars fell from the sky and moved into her breast.

The Marquess's kiss lasted for what seemed an eternity before he said:

"This is what I have been looking for. This is love, my Precious."

Then he was kissing her again, kissing her demandingly, possessively, until she was no longer herself, but a part of him.

It was impossible to think, impossible to breathe.

At last the Marquess said in a strange, deep voice that sounded a little unsteady:

"I love you! I love you, Athina, and I had no idea that I could feel as I do at this moment."

"Y-you . . . love me . . . you really . . . love . . . me?" Athina whispered.

"I adore you, I worship you! You are everything I have always wanted, and the reason why I had no wish to marry anyone was that I did not believe that anyone like you really existed."

He kissed the tears away from her eyes before he said:

"Now tell me that you love me too."

"I did not . . . know what . . . love was like,"

Athina said. "But now I know . . . that it is glorious . . . wonderful! And . . . how . . . could I not . . . love you?"

"You told me I was the last man in the world you would marry," the Marquess reminded her, "but you are going to marry me, my lovely one, because I cannot live without you."

"I . . . I thought I . . . hated you," Athina confessed, "because you had neglected Peter . . . but now I know how wonderfully clever and kind you are . . . and I love . . . you more . . . than I can . . . ever say."

"And I love you," the Marquess said. "My Darling, how could we imagine we would find each other in such a strange fashion?"

She knew he was thinking that if she had not been obliged to stay at the Posting-Inn, they might never have met.

If she had not befriended Peter, who happened to be in the room which communicated with hers, she would not have known he was the Marquess's nephew.

It all seemed like a weird and complicated puzzle.

Yet Fate had brought two people together who had loathed the idea of being married.

The thought passed through both their minds.

Then the Marquess asked:

"How soon will you marry me? I have no intention of waiting. I want you now, at once, and I am so desperately afraid of losing you."

"You will . . . never lose . . . me," Athina said, "and . . . I will . . . marry you . . . whenever you . . . wish."

The Marquess pulled her closer to him before he answered.

"I would marry you at this very moment if I could."

The moonlight shone on her face, and he looked down at her lingeringly before he said:

"How can you be so utterly beautiful? But it is much more than that. You are everything I want in a woman, everything I dreamt a woman should be like. But I was convinced she existed only in my imagination."

"I . . . I am . . . afraid I may . . . disappoint you," Athina whispered. "I knew when I . . . came to your room . . . tonight and . . . saw you asleep that . . . you were not only the most . . . handsome man I have . . . ever seen, but also too . . . marvellous to be . . . human."

The Marquess laughed.

"I assure you, my Darling, I am very human when I kiss you and want you to be mine. At the same time, we each recognise in the other something that is different."

He paused for a moment. Then he said quietly:

"I believe God made us for each other, and that is why our love is different from what it would ever be with anybody else."

"How can you . . . say such . . . marvellous things . . . to me?" Athina asked. "Things I have . . . thought in . . . my heart . . . but never . . . imagined a man would . . . say them."

The Marquess drew in his breath.

"We have a great deal to learn about each other," he said, "and therefore the sooner we are married, the better."

Athina moved a little closer to him.

"Could we," she asked hesitatingly, "just be . . . married here in the country? Either in the village Church where I was . . . baptised . . . or perhaps in your Private Chapel which I have not yet seen, although I know you have one."

"Would that make you happy?" the Marquess asked.

"I would be happy . . . anywhere with . . . you," Athina answered, "but I am afraid that what we are feeling now is just . . . part of the . . . moonlight and a wonderful . . . wonderful dream."

She hid her face against his neck as she said:

"I have lived . . . quietly in the . . . country and . . . know nothing . . . of London. I am . . . afraid of your . . . smart friends. If they . . . laughed or sniggered . . . it would . . . spoil what we are . . . feeling . . . now."

She spoke so softly that the Marquess could hardly hear what she was saying.

Then his arms tightened round her and he said:

"You are quite right and that is what I feel myself. We will be married here in my private Chapel by my Chaplain, who is also the Vicar of the Parish."

He smiled at her before he went on:

"And the only witnesses to our wedding will be Peter and Mrs. Beckwith."

"Peter will be . . . thrilled," Athina said.

Then she gave a little exclamation.

"Oh, Denzil, is it true . . . really . . . true that we need no longer be . . . afraid for . . . him? I know it is . . . only a matter of days . . . but I feel . . . we have been . . . fighting for him for . . . years. Because you are the Knight of Chivalry who I thought existed only in books, is he now . . . safe and . . . need . . . never be . . . afraid again?"

She felt as if the words tumbled from her mouth and she had no control over them.

The Marquess did not answer.

He merely kissed her until once again they were with the stars and no longer on earth.

He knew it had been a long search to find a woman who could take his Mother's place at Rock.

Athina filled the shrine in his heart which he had hesitated to admit was there, even to himself.

He had found her.

She was young, unspoilt, and very innocent.

Their love, he knew, was ageless and came from eternity and would go on to eternity.

It was the glory and wonder he had been sure he would never find.

"This is love," he said again as he carried Athina up into the sky.

ABOUT THE AUTHOR

Barbara Cartland, the world's most famous romantic novelist, who is also an historian, playwright, lecturer, political speaker and television personality, has now written over 587 books and sold over six hundred and twenty million copies all over the world.

She has also had many historical works published and has written four autobiographies as well as the biographies of her mother and that of her brother, Ronald Cartland, who was the first Member of Parliament to be killed in the last war. This book has a preface by Sir Winston Churchill and has just been republished with an introduction by Sir Arthur Bryant.

Love at the Helm, a novel written with the help and inspiration of the late Earl Mountbatten of Burma, Great Uncle of His Royal Highness, The Prince of Wales, is being sold for the Mountbatten Memorial Trust.

She has broken the world record for the last nineteen years by writing an average of twenty-three books a year. In the *Guinness Book of World Records* she is listed as the world's top-selling author.

Miss Cartland in 1987 sang an Album of Love Songs with the Royal Philharmonic Orchestra.

In private life Barbara Cartland, who is a Dame of the Order of St. John of Jerusalem, Chairman of the St. John Council in Hertfordshire and Deputy President of the St. John Ambulance Brigade, has fought for better conditions and salaries for Midwives and Nurses.

She championed the cause for the Elderly in 1956 invoking a Government Enquiry into the "Housing Condition of Old People."

In 1962 she had the Law of England changed so that Local Authorities had to provide camps for their own Gypsies. This has meant that since then thousands and thousands of Gypsy children have been able to go to School, which they had never been able to do in the past, as their caravans were moved every twenty-four hours by the Police.

There are now fourteen camps in Hertfordshire and Barbara Cartland has her own Romany Gypsy Camp called Barbaraville by the Gypsies.

Her designs "Decorating with Love" are being sold all over the U.S.A. and the National Home Fashions League made her, in 1981, "Woman of Achievement."

She is unique in that she was one and two in the Dalton list of Best Sellers, and one week had four books in the top twenty.

Barbara Cartland's book *Getting Older, Growing Younger* has been published in Great Britain and the U.S.A. and her fifth cookery book, *The Romance of Food*, is now being used by the House of Commons.

In 1984 she received at Kennedy Airport America's Bishop Wright Air Industry Award for her contribution to the development of aviation. In 1931 she and two R.A.F. Officers thought of, and carried, the first aeroplane-towed glider airmail.

During the War she was Chief Lady Welfare Officer in Bedfordshire, looking after 20,000 Servicemen and -women. She thought of having a pool of Wedding Dresses at the war office so a Service Bride could hire a gown for the day.

She bought 1,000 gowns without coupons for the A.T.S., the W.A.A.F.'s and the W.R.E.N.S. In 1945 Barbara Cartland received the Certificate of Merit from Eastern Command.

In 1964 Barbara Cartland founded the National Association for Health of which she is the President, as a front for all the Health Stores and for any product made as alternative medicine.

This is now a £65 million turnover a year, with one-third going in export.

In January 1968 she received *La Médeille de Vermeil de la Ville de Paris*. This is the highest award to be given in France by the City of Paris. She has sold 25 million books in France.

In March 1988 Barbara Cartland was asked by the Indian Government to open their Health Resort outside Delhi. This is almost the largest Health Resort in the world.

Barbara Cartland was received with great enthusiasm by her fans, who feted her at a reception in the City, and she received the gift of an embossed plate from the Government.

Barbara Cartland was made a Dame of the Order of the British Empire in the 1991 New Year's Honours List by Her Majesty, The Queen, for her contribution to Literature and also for her years of work for the community.

Dame Barbara has now written the greatest number of books by a British author, passing the 564 books written by John Creasey.

AWARDS

1945   Received Certificate of Merit, Eastern Command, for being Welfare Officer to 5,000 troops in Bedfordshire.

1953   Made a Commander of the Order of St. John of Jerusalem. Invested by H.R.H. The Duke of Gloucester at Buckingham Palace.

1972   Invested as Dame of Grace of the Order of St. John in London by The Lord Prior, Lord Cacia.

1981   Received "Achiever of the Year" from the National Home Furnishing Association in Colorado Springs, U.S.A., for her designs for wallpaper and fabrics.

1984   Received Bishop Wright Air Industry Award at Kennedy Airport, for inventing the aeroplane-towed Glider.

1988   Received from Monsieur Chirac, The Prime Minister, The Gold Medal of the City of Paris, at the Hotel de la Ville, Paris, for selling 25 million books and giving a lot of employment.

1991   Invested as Dame of the Order of The British Empire, by H.M. The Queen at Buckingham Palace for her contribution to Literature.